If Only Love Could Last

by Janet Adele Bloss

I dedicate this book with heartfelt love to my sister Terry, her husband Bob, and to their children, Jonathon and Andrew.

Cover photo by Bichsel Morris
Photographic Illustrators

One

"BUT, Mom!" Hilary wailed. "I don't want to move. I love Philadelphia. I can't leave my friends! What about Mike? What's he going to say?"

Edith Weathervan looked down at her daughter sympathetically. "I know, Hon," she said. "It's hard. I'm leaving all my friends, too. But the company's moving me to the home office in Massachusetts. It's a promotion and I'll be making more money. Now that we don't have your dad's salary to count on anymore, it's more important than ever that I take my career seriously."

Hilary twisted a finger in her short blonde hair. "Mom, couldn't we just ask Dad for some more child support money?" she asked.

Mrs. Weathervan patted her daughter's shoulder. "He's paying his fair share," she said. "I can't complain. But now that your dad and I are divorced and he's moved to Montana, well, it's just you and me, kid."

Hilary's mom winked at her and smiled.

Moving! Hilary thought. They were moving from Philadelphia, Pennsylvania, to some little rinky dink town in Massachusetts called Suffington. "What could be worse?" she muttered. "It wouldn't be so bad if I wasn't leaving Mike."

Mike Dillow was a boy Hilary had known since first grade. They'd grown up together, and they'd always been friends. But their friendship had changed somehow in the last year or so. It wasn't such a tag-along friendship anymore. It was more special. They weren't sitting in a sandbox throwing sand like they used to. No, now Mike gave Hilary his jacket when they were caught in a rainstorm together, and there were days when Hilary couldn't even look at Mike without feeling her face become flushed. There were lots of little things like that. But they added up to a big thing, a big and lovely friendship. Hilary wondered what Mike would say when he heard the news.

* * * * *

Mike and Hilary walked down the city street together. They stopped at the corner where a vendor in a white uniform stood by a cart full of soft pretzels. Mike bought two and gave one to Hilary. She squirted mustard on it then bit

4

into the warm, chewy dough. Little grains of salt melted on her tongue. The mustard tasted spicy. Traffic droned by as they walked down the sidewalk. Pigeons sat along the window-sills and roof edges of towering buildings. All kinds of people hurried by — punkers with mohawks and blue hair, ladies in magazine-fashion dresses, men in suits, mothers pushing strollers. There was always something happening in the city. It was as if you could feel the city breathing with life.

Mike and Hilary approached the large, stone structure that was their junior high school. It stood on a corner of the street across from several business offices. The school stretched for almost a full city block. Mike and Hilary looked up at the school and all sorts of shared memories came rushing over them. "What am I going to do without you?" asked Mike. He looked into Hilary's hazel eyes.

Hilary shook her head. "I don't know," she said. "What am I going to do in some strange town with no friends and no you?" she asked.

Mike shrugged. "Well, maybe I can take a bus up and visit you on holidays. Anyway, I know you'll write lots of letters," he said.

Hilary laughed. Mike was right. He knew she'd write a lot because Hilary loved to write. She wrote for the school newspaper and she wanted to be a writer when she grew up. She had a notebook full of poems that she was working on. Someday Hilary planned to send them to *Seventeen* Magazine and try to get them published.

"I'll write all the time," Hilary promised. "I'll try to write every day. I probably won't have anything else to do anyway," she said, grinning. "I won't know anyone to do anything with."

"I'll call you whenever I can," Mike said. "I'll write, too. But you know I don't write as well as you do. So, probably I'll spend most of my time on the phone. I'll call you every Friday night at 7:30, okay?"

"Okay," said Hilary. She and Mike held hands as they walked back to Hilary's home.

That night Hilary called Sharon Kelt, the editor of the school newspaper. Hilary turned in her resignation and suggested that Paul Withers take her place writing for the paper.

*   *   *   *   *

The movers came the next week and went through the Weathervans' house packing lamps and dishes into boxes. Hilary felt like crying as she saw her home slowly disappear around her. The carpet was rolled up and carried to a van. The pictures were removed from the living room, leaving squares of lighter

6

paint on the walls behind them. Suddenly, her home wasn't her home anymore.

It wouldn't have been so bad if Dad was here, Hilary thought. But he wasn't. Now that her parents were divorced, it seemed like everything was changing. First her dad was gone. Now all their familiar furniture wasn't there. In just two days Hilary and her mom would be gone, too. Everything seemed to be disappearing. Soon, just a shell of a house would be left.

Hilary's last two days in Philadelphia went by quickly. At last her final day in Philadelphia arrived. She stood with Mike, holding hands, on the front porch of the Weathervans' empty house. A September sun glittered from the windows of cars parked up and down the street.

"Well, this is it," Mike said. "I'm going to miss you. Be sure and write."

"I will," Hilary said, holding back the tears. "I'll write every day. Don't forget me." Mike smiled as if to say that forgetting Hilary would be impossible.

"Come on, Hon," Hilary's mom said. "Let's get this show on the road. Mike, I hope you'll come visit us."

Hilary climbed into the car beside her mother. She stared out the window at Mike who was standing alone and looking forlorn on the porch. He waved. Hilary waved back as her mom drove the car out from the curb into traffic. As they drove away, Mike dwindled to a little speck. Then the car turned a corner and Mike was lost from sight.

Hilary began to sniffle. "Oh, Mom," she cried. "Why does it have to be like this? Why can't you stay in Philadelphia and work?"

"Honey, you know the company is growing," her mom said. "I'm being transferred out there because it's a farm community. Since we sell farm machinery and I'm a market analyst, it's very important for me to be aware of what the farmers' needs are. I need to find new markets for our merchandise. You know, new places where we can sell our stuff. Since Planters' Friend, Inc. is the name of the company, I'd better get out there and be a planter's friend. How am I going to know where we should advertise our stuff if I'm not closer to the people who might need it?"

"Can't you be a planter's friend in Philadelphia?" asked Hilary.

"Sorry, Hon. This is a city. Suffington is a dairy farm and grain producing area. It's a nice little town. I think you'll like it once you get used to it and make some friends."

But Hilary wasn't so sure about making friends. She never really had to worry about friends in Philadelphia. She worked on the school newspaper and that took a lot of her time. Then Mike took up the rest of it. He was her best friend. But now she wouldn't have Mike anymore.

Sometimes Hilary wished that her mother didn't take her job so seriously. She wished her mom was the kind of mom who spent the afternoon baking brownies. Instead, Edith Weathervan was the kind of mom who got up at 5:30 in the morning, made breakfast, and left the house looking very businesslike in a navy blue suit. Her mom was the kind who stayed up until midnight going through her work papers, looking at columns of numbers.

It was hard sometimes for Hilary to hug or talk to her mom. Her mom was either too busy, or her suit looked too stiff. It would've been a lot easier to hug a mom who wore a flowered cotton dress.

As the car left the city, Hilary watched the landscape begin to change. The land became hilly and forests lined the road. Autumn colors prevailed with golden-orange maples and browning oaks nodding in the crisp breeze. Masses of tiny yellow flowers climbed the grassy strip that divided the highway. Hilary and her mom stopped for lunch, then they were on the road again. Hours passed. With Philadelphia getting further away, Hilary felt as if she was falling into a bottomless hole. It

9

was a hole of uncertainty and fright.

Their car sped past a large green sign that said "Welcome to Massachusetts." Hilary's mom honked the horn and said, "Excellent! We're almost there!"

Hilary felt awful. She stared out the window for a while, then tried to sleep. It seemed like ages. Finally as the evening light spread over the countryside, they passed a sign that said "Suffington — 9 Miles." Hilary sat up in her seat preparing herself for her first look at her new hometown. The car crested a hill and Hilary looked down on the scene before her.

"Oh, no!" she gasped. "Mom, are you kidding? We're going to live here? Where's the town? Where are the buildings? Where are the soft pretzel vendors? Where's all the traffic? Don't they have buses in this town?"

Hilary looked around and what she saw, or rather didn't see, amazed her. "Where are the parks?" she asked. "This town would fit into Philadelphia's back pocket!"

Mrs. Weathervan looked wryly at her daughter. "I think, my dear, that things are going to be a little different here," she said. "They don't have parks like we have in Philadelphia. There's one little park that they call the 'town square.' It's really quite nice. There are trees all over the place. We have a couple of trees in our backyard, too, and

10

there's a woods just down the road. Wait until you see our house. I think you'll like it. It's a lot bigger than what we could afford in Philadelphia."

Mrs. Weathervan had visited Suffington several weeks earlier when she was there to find a house and to tour the home office facility. "Look!" she said. "That's where I'll be working." They drove by a six-story brick building which was the biggest building in the town. There was a big sign in front that said "Planters' Friend, Inc." A picture of a farmer holding an ear of corn was beside the words.

Hilary's stomach felt like a hard knot of wood. She looked around at the town. Where was it? she wondered. It wasn't anything like Philadelphia. This town would not only fit in Philadelphia's back pocket, there would be plenty of room left over!

"Look, Hilary!" said her mom. "That's where you'll be going to school."

Hilary looked at a three-story brick building. The sign on the front lawn said "Suffington High School."

"That can't be it," said Hilary. "I'm in junior high school. That sign says 'High School.' "

"I know, dear," said Hilary's mom. "But this is a small town. They've put the junior and senior high schools into one building. The grade school is just down the road."

Hilary couldn't believe it. Here was a town that was so small that they only had one high school. Not only that, but it was crammed into the same building with the junior high school. But in Philadelphia they had hundreds of junior high school buildings, Hilary recalled, frowning.

"Here's our house," Mrs. Weathervan said. "How do you like it?" She pulled the car into the driveway beside a large white-shingled house. Wooden lace edged the roof.

"Wow!" exclaimed Hilary. "Is it all ours or do we live in half of it?"

Edith Weathervan laughed. "It's all ours, Hon. It's big, isn't it?"

Hilary jumped from the car and ran up the front porch. Her mom hurried behind her, pulling the key out of her purse. She opened the front door and the two of them rushed in. A large living room stretched to the right of them and the dining room was to the left. A staircase wound up to the second floor. There were large windows in every room and pink light from the setting sun streamed in.

"Wow!" Hilary gasped again. "Wait until Mike sees this. He'll love it!"

A little later the moving van pulled up in front of the house. The workmen began carrying in furniture and Mrs. Weathervan told them where to put it. "The couch goes there," she said. "And put that china hutch in the dining room on the short wall. Yes, that's it. Good. That's Hilary's desk. It goes in the blue room on the second floor."

Hilary followed the movers up to her room. It was big with a window facing the backyard.

"Where do you want this desk to go, little lady?" asked one of the movers.

"By the window, please," answered Hilary. The men set the desk down and left the room to get more furniture. Hilary sat at the desk and gazed out the window into scarlet-leaved branches. Beyond the branches was a picket fence which separated the Weathervans' yard from the yard behind them. A two-story gray house could be seen in the fading light.

As Hilary looked at the gray house she thought she saw a movement at a second-floor window. She looked more closely and thought she could see the shadowy outline of a figure standing next to the window. Eyes seemed to be watching her. Who was it? she wondered. Hilary leaned forward to get a better view, but the figure moved backward and disappeared into the dark room. Maybe it's just my imagination, she thought. Maybe it was just the shadows of the trees moving across the house.

That night Hilary and her mother went out for dinner because it was too late to shop for groceries. If they'd been in Philadelphia, they could have chosen from hundreds of restaurants, cafes, and delicatessens. But Suffington could offer only a little restaurant called "The Suffington Inn." Hilary couldn't believe how small the menu was. There were few choices. She was hoping that there would be a Chinese or an Italian restaurant. But it was the Suffington Inn or nothing.

Back at the house, Hilary unpacked her clothes and arranged her closet and drawers. She put her makeup case on her dresser and chose the lip gloss she would wear on her first day of school. It was a pink lilac color. It would look nice with the the purple and white outfit she was planning to wear. It was an outfit that had been advertised in the August issue of *Seventeen*.

Then Hilary sat at her desk and began writing on a strawberry-scented sheet of paper. She wrote:

September 23

Dear Mike,

You would not believe this town. It's so small that I thought only midgets could live here. But I saw some regular people downtown when we drove in. Speaking of downtown, it's incredible! There

14

are only four or five stores. There's only one restaurant and only one high school!

The nicest thing is our house. It's huge compared to the one in Philly. All the houses around here seem pretty large. Mom says that they're all about eighty years old. I guess people just used to have huge houses.

I start school tomorrow. Yuk! I dread it. But hopefully I won't be too far behind or anything. The first thing I'm going to do is find out if this rinky dink school has a newspaper I can write for.

You wouldn't believe how many cows live around this place. We drove by hundreds of them on the way in. I'm still kind of mad at my mom for making me move here. The house is nice, but the town is so small that it's ridiculous.

I'd better go to bed now. Tomorrow's a big day. I can't wait for you to call this Friday. Don't forget. I'll be waiting by the phone at 7:30 like you said.

I miss you and I'm going to try to
dream about you tonight. Bye.

Love,

Hilary

Hilary switched off her desk lamp and put
on her pajamas. It was fun to be in a dark
room. She thought about turning off all the
lights and walking around the house. She
would walk down the hall with her hand
touching the wall. Sometimes Hilary liked to
walk around in the darkness. To Hilary
everything seemed to have softer edges in the
dark.

With her pajamas on, Hilary walked to her
bedroom window for a last look at her new
yard. She looked beyond the trees to the gray
house. Something moved! she thought. Or was
it her imagination? Once again, it seemed as if
the curtains had shivered at the upstairs
window. Hilary stared into the darkness. Was
someone standing there? Was someone
watching her? Brrr-r-r, she thought. It gave her
the creeps to think about it. Why would
someone hide behind the curtains and spy on
her?

Hilary crawled into bed. A New England
wind whistled around the house, shaking the
shutters and rattling the windows. It was a

little cooler here than it was in Philadelphia, and Hilary pulled the blankets up snuggly under her chin. She thought about the new school she would be attending the next day. And she tried not to think about it. It was scary.

Then she thought about Mike and began to drift off to sleep. She thought about the good times they'd had together, walking through Bowman Park, wading in the fountain, feeding the pigeons. She wondered how soon Mike would come for a visit. She thought about the phone call she could expect on Friday. "Oh, well," she sighed. At least there was one thing to look forward to. But suddenly, a new thought inched its way into Hilary's brain. "We don't have a phone!" Hilary whispered to herself. "It hasn't been hooked up yet."

Oh, great, Hilary thought. Here I am in the middle of nowhere. I might as well be in Alaska. It's like I don't even exist.

But someone did know that Hilary was in Suffington. Someone had seen her move into the big white-shingled house. And someone had watched her as she sat at her desk writing a letter to Mike. That same someone still stood by the second-floor window and continued to watch, while Hilary slept.

Two

HILARY'S first day of school wasn't nearly as bad as she thought it would be. The kids were friendly. In fact, Hilary suddenly felt like a fashion model in her purple and white skirt and sweater. You would have thought she was wearing a dress from Mars from the way the other students reacted to her outfit. They stared at her and complimented her every time she turned around. At least, it seemed that way. When she was in the restroom combing her hair between first and second periods, a group of girls gathered beside her in front of the mirror. "I love your lip gloss," said one of them.

"Wow!" another girl said. "If I wore my skirts that short, my mom would skin me alive. Where'd you get it?"

"Philadelphia," said Hilary. "That's where I'm from. My name's Hilary Weathervan."

"What a pretty name," said a girl wearing glasses. "I'm Pam Smith."

"I'm Bonnie Jean Kite," said another one.

"I'm Jerry Dapple," said a girl with freckles. "Wow! Triple-pierced ears! Neat! Does everyone in Philadelphia have triple-pierced ears?"

"Just about," said Hilary. "Some of the guys only have single-pierced, though." She noticed that the other girls only had single-pierced ears, except for Jerry. Her ears weren't pierced at all.

"Does everyone in Philadelphia wear mini-skirts?" asked Bonnie Jean.

"Just about," Hilary said again. She noticed that the hemlines around her reached to the tops of knees. They were a good deal longer than her own hemline. Hilary applied lilac-pink lip gloss to her lips, while the other girls watched.

"Neat color," said Pam.

"Thanks," said Hilary. She was beginning to feel like a movie star. Maybe I should offer to give out autographs, she giggled to herself. The kids in this town act like they've never met anyone from a big city before, she thought.

At lunch time, Hilary was invited to sit at a table with Pam, Bonnie Jean, Jerry and some other kids. They asked her questions about Philadelphia and about herself, such as what she liked to do.

"I like to write," said Hilary. "I worked on the school newspaper at my school in Philly. Is there a paper here?"

"Sure," said Bonnie Jean. "It's the *Suffington Sentinel.* It comes out once every two weeks. If you want to work on it, just ask Dan Ellsworth. He's the editor. He's a real nice guy. He's the one over there in the gray sweater-vest."

Hilary followed the direction of Bonnie Jean's pointed finger to a brown-haired boy sitting at another table. His glasses were perched atop his nose. He appeared to be a serious student, maybe even a little bit of a brain. Hilary hoped he'd let her work on the paper.

After lunch, Hilary had math, then science class. She could tell just from one day at school that she wasn't behind in her studies. In fact, she was slightly ahead in math and she was definitely ahead in English.

It seemed weird to be in a school with seventh and twelfth graders. It wasn't so great to be in the youngest class in a school where the oldest students were five years older. But the fact that Hilary dressed differently and wore brighter makeup helped her to look older than the other seventh graders.

When the last bell of the day rang, Hilary gathered her books together and left the school building. On the steps outside she saw Dan Ellsworth, also with an armload of books.

"Excuse me!" called Hilary

Dan looked at her with surprise.

"Excuse me!" Hilary called again, hurrying over to Dan's side. "I'm Hilary Weathervan. I just moved here from Philadelphia. I heard you are editor of the school paper and I'd like to work on it. I'm a very good writer and I used to work on the school paper in Philly."

Dan's mouth slowly moved into a smile as he listened to Hilary. "So, you're a very good writer, huh?" he joked.

Suddenly, Hilary felt a little bashful. "Well, I think I am," she said. "I write all the time."

"Well, we really need someone to work on the sports section," said Dan. "Think you could handle that?"

"Sports?" Hilary gasped. "Well-l-l, sure. I just love sports." Hilary wondered if Dan could tell that she was fibbing. Hilary didn't know the first thing about sports. But she figured that if she was ever going to be a professional writer, she'd better learn to take any writing assignment she was given, even if that meant learning about sports.

"You can start with the football game next Saturday night," said Dan. "You cover that story and turn it in to me. I'll run it by Mr. Rafferty. He's the journalism teacher and advisor for the school newspaper. If it's okay with him, then you can be on the staff. Okay?"

"Great!" said Hilary. "Thanks a lot. I'll do my very best. See you later." She clutched her books to herself and walked down the steps. Then she turned toward home.

Her first day had gone well enough. Hilary thought the clothes here were so out-of-date. And didn't the girls know that short-short hair was in? she wondered. Living in a small town really must make people blind to style and fashion. Hilary hoped that she wouldn't live in Suffington long enough to get that way. Well, maybe as long as she kept her subscription to *Seventeen* she'd be okay. That was her one link with the outside, civilized world of fashion.

Hilary walked home and let herself in with her key. Her mother would be home in two hours. That gave Hilary plenty of time to change her clothes, write to Mike, and unpack some boxes. She sat at her desk and wrote:

Dear Mike,

I miss you more than ever. Today was my first day of school and the kids were nice, but they're kind of jerky, if you know what I mean. They dress like they are behind in the times.

Also, there's no museum in this town. I checked it out on the way home. I'm beginning to feel like Daniel Boone in the wilderness. There's nothing to do here. Mom says our phone will be in this Saturday.

Here's a short poem I wrote in study hall today.

Suffering in Sufferington

Nothing to do and nowhere to go.
I can't believe I've sunk this low
As to move to a town that's full of
*   cows*
And farmers on tractors pulling their
*   ploughs.*
I may go nuts. I may go mad.
I might move to Montana to live
*   with my dad.*

Anyway, this is a weird, dinky little town. I'll write tomorrow. Bye.

Love,
Hilary

Hilary read the letter a final time and placed it in an envelope. Then she walked downstairs to the kitchen to unpack boxes of dishes.

A click-click-click sound came from the

brass door-knocker on the front door. Hilary stood and brushed the dust from her jeans. Then she walked to the front hall and opened the door.

Pam Smith, Bonnie Jean Kite, and Jerry Dapple stood on the porch. Jerry's round, freckled face showed a cheerful smile.

"Hi, Hilary! We just thought we'd walk over and visit you. Can we come in?" Jerry asked.

"Sure," laughed Hilary. "Come on in. The house is kind of a wreck, though. We're still unpacking. How did you know where I lived?"

The three girls looked at each other and began to giggle.

"The whole town knows when someone new moves into Suffington," explained Pam. "My mom found out from the Garden Club. I don't know where they found out. But I heard that there was a girl my age moving into this house."

"I heard that your mom works for Planters' Friend, Inc." said Bonnie Jean. "My dad's a farmer. He's hoping that Planters' Friend will make the prices of tractors come down."

"This was the only house for sale near the high school, so we figured you'd move here," said Jerry, flipping her hair back off her shoulders. "Then when they took the FOR SALE sign down a week ago, we knew for sure that this was going to be your house. Everyone in the whole school has been expecting you."

"Yeah," nodded Pam. "It's a real big deal when someone new moves into town."

Hilary led the three girls up the stairs to her blue bedroom. They sat down and continued to chat. Hilary noticed that the scarf around Pam's neck didn't quite match her sweater. If it was Hilary's scarf, she would have ripped it into two pieces and tied them at her ankles at the bottom of her soft cotton baggies. Everyone in Philly was wearing long bloomers, but the style didn't seem to have reached Suffington yet.

"Did you talk to Dan Ellsworth?" asked Pam.

"Yeah." Hilary thought back to the brown-haired boy in the gray sweater-vest. "He needs someone to work on sports articles," she said, wrinkling her nose. "I don't know much about sports, but I'm supposed to do a story on the football game this Saturday. I hope it won't be too boring."

"Boring?" cried Bonnie Jean. "Anything but boring! We have one of the best football teams in the whole state!"

"No kidding!" said Pam. "The players are really great! What you should do is interview the players after the game. They'll give you plenty to write about."

Suddenly the three girls from Suffington

began to grin mischievously.

"I know who I'd interview, if I had half a chance," said Pam.

"No, you wouldn't, 'cause I'd interview him first," laughed Jerry.

"Who?" asked Hilary.

All three girls exclaimed at once, "Eddie Stoner!" Then there was a flurry of sighing and giggling.

Hilary felt a little embarrassed. Giggling about boys was not something that Hilary did, or had ever done for that matter. She didn't have to because there had always been Mike. Hilary never really even noticed other boys.

"Who's Eddie Stoner?" asked Hilary.

"He's *only* the captain of the Junior Varsity football team!" cried Jerry.

"And he's *only* the cutest guy in the eighth grade!" shrieked Pam. "He's a year older than we are."

"You'll die when you meet him," sighed Bonnie Jean. "I can't believe you get to interview him this Friday. Wow! Of all the luck!"

Hilary smiled. She wondered to herself about how great this Eddie guy could be. If he was like all the other people in this town, he was probably a little weird, and he probably wore terrible clothes. Hopefully, he wouldn't smell like a cow, the way some of the farm kids did. In fact, Hilary could smell a slight scent of cow on Bonnie Jean.

Just then the front door could be heard opening and Edith Weathervan called, "Hilary! I'm home!"

Hilary took her new friends downstairs to meet her mother. She was wearing a gray wool suit with a cream-colored silk blouse.

"It's nice to meet you, girls," said Mrs. Weathervan. "Won't you stay for dinner?"

"What are we having?" asked Hilary.

"I thought I'd send out for some fried chicken and mashed potatoes," said Hilary's mom. "I just discovered a little carry-out on the way home."

"Thank you, but I can't," said Bonnie Jean. "My mom's expecting me and it's kind of late to spoil her dinner plans. I'd better be going."

"Me, too," said Pam and Jerry.

Hilary thought to herself about how other mothers cooked regular meals with tons of food. But her mom invited people over for carry-out food. That's what happens when you have a working mother, she thought. Probably the other girls' moms stayed home and cooked and cleaned and took care of their families. But not *my* mom. She was too busy carrying around briefcases and making sure her solar cell calculator worked.

Hilary walked with the three girls outside to

the front porch. They promised to meet together in the school cafeteria for lunch the next day. As they began to leave, Hilary thought of a question that had been lurking in her brain all day.

"Who lives in the big gray house behind me? she asked. "I keep thinking I see someone at a top floor window watching me."

"Are you serious?" asked Jerry. Suddenly her face lost all its smiles and became very serious.

"Did you actually see her?" asked Pam.

"See who?" asked Hilary. "That's what I want to know. Who lives there?"

"That's Old Lady Suffington's house," said Bonnie Jean. "The town was named after her husband's grandfather, Zachary Suffington. She's real old. Her husband died about a million years ago."

"What's she like?" asked Hilary.

"No one knows," Bonnie Jean said, shaking her head. "She has her groceries delivered and she hasn't been out of the house in years. I've never seen her. Ever since her husband died she hides away in that big, dark house."

"That's weird," said Hilary. "Why does she do it?"

"She's nuts," said Bonnie Jean.

"Absolutely cuckoo," whispered Pam, looking nervously around her. "They say all

28

her hair and teeth have fallen out and she's forgotten how to talk."

"She's as crazy as they come," said Jerry. "I wouldn't mess with her if I were you."

Hilary thought of the second floor window in the big gray house. She remembered when she'd seen the curtains by that window flutter, then fall still. A dark form had hovered in the darker room beyond the window.

"She's nuts," Bonnie Jean called from the gate as she left the Weathervan home. Evening darkness was falling and Hilary heard Bonnie Jean's voice drift back softly from down the road, ". . . Absolutely nuts."

Three

"HI, Hilary. Boy, I miss you. This old city just isn't the same without you."

Mike's voice sounded clear and strong over the telephone. It was six o'clock on Saturday evening.

"I tried to call last night like I promised, but your phone must not have been hooked up yet."

"Right," said Hilary. "We just got it in this morning. You're my very first telephone call. Guess what! I think I'm getting a job on the newspaper staff. It's not nearly as big as the paper in Philly, but it's better than nothing."

"What section are you working on?" asked Mike.

Hilary drew in a little breath, then said, "Sports. Can you believe it?"

"I didn't know you liked sports," said Mike.

"I don't," said Hilary. "But it's a writing job and I'll take what I can get. My first assignment is tonight. I'm covering a football game at school. Can you believe it?"

Mike laughed softly. He and Hilary continued to talk and it made Hilary feel like crying to hear his voice so far away. But the conversation ended on a happy note when Mike promised he'd spend Thanksgiving at the Weathervan home in Suffington. That was two long months away, but at least she could look forward to his visit.

They said good-bye and Hilary kept the phone to her ear after Mike hung up. There were several clicks, then a dial tone. Hilary felt as if she were listening into a great, empty piece of time. She hung up.

Then Hilary went to her room to dress for the football game. First she pulled down the window shade. She was always careful to do that ever since she heard about the crazy Mrs. Suffington who lived behind her. Hilary wondered with a smile if it was the smallness of the town that had driven Mrs. Suffington crazy. But then she shivered again, thinking about the strange toothless old woman who spent her life hiding in the dark.

Hilary pulled on a pair of cherry red slacks that hugged and complimented her slender hips and legs. Then over her head she pulled a short-waisted gray lamb's wool sweater. It was as soft as a kitten's fur and brought out the pink blush of her cheeks. Short black suede boots complemented the outfit.

Then Hilary put a pearl stud, an onyx stud and a red dangly earring in each ear. She applied creamy crimson lip gloss to her lips, pulled a comb through her short blonde hair and she was ready to go. Hilary grabbed a jacket, her pen and an interview notebook, and descended the stairs.

"My! Don't you look nice!" her mom exclaimed. "Are you sure you don't want me to go with you?" she asked.

"No thanks, Mom," said Hilary. "Bonnie Jean's dad is driving us. We're meeting Jerry and Pam at the game. Bonnie Jean said her dad would give me a ride home, too."

A small truck pulled up into the driveway, its headlights flashing into the living room.

"Bye," called Hilary.

"Good luck on your interview," called Mrs. Weathervan.

Hilary ran out the door and climbed into the truck's front seat with Bonnie Jean and her father. Hilary quietly rolled the window down just a crack as the warm, earthy smell of cows invaded her nostrils.

"Wow! You look great!" exclaimed Bonnie Jean. "But then you always do. This is my dad. Dad, this is Hilary Weathervan."

"How do, young lady," said Mr. Kite. "I've been hearing a good deal about you lately.

You'll have to come out to the farm sometime and see our stock."

"He means our cows and horses," explained Bonnie Jean.

Mr. Kite pulled into the school parking lot. Other cars, pickup trucks, and buses surrounded them.

"Why don't you gals run along?" asked Mr. Kite. "I'll pick you up after the game."

Hilary, then Bonnie Jean, jumped down from the truck's cab. Hilary bent over and brushed dirt from the tops of her boots. Then she followed Bonnie Jean through the parking lot to the football field.

Huge white lights cut through the autumn night, illuminating the green field with straight white lines. Brass instruments glittered in the band section of the bleachers. The smell of popcorn and earth filled the brisk air and mingled with sounds of laughter, shouting, and conversation.

Hilary felt as if she were walking into a three-ring circus. Kids ran by and students seated in the stands held paper cups of hot chocolate between their mittened hands.

"Here we are! Here we are!" yelled Jerry and Pam.

Bonnie Jean and Hilary spotted them sitting in the sixth row of bleachers on the 50-yard line. Hilary climbed up behind Bonnie Jean

33

and wedged into the row. The excitement around her caused her breathing to quicken. As Hilary sat, surveying the football field, she sensed heads turning to look at her. Boys and girls throughout the crowd wanted to see the "new girl."

Suddenly the brass drum began pounding and the crowd began roaring. The Suffington Sentries ran onto the field in their green and white uniforms. Hilary wondered which one was Eddie Stoner. From this distance, they all looked alike with smudges of black under their eyes.

As if reading her mind, Pam whispered, "He's number 11. See? He's leading the pack."

Indeed he was. Strong legs in white pants flickered as number 11 ran onto the field at the head of the team.

The visiting team ran onto the field from the opposite end and muffled shouting could be heard from the other stands. The band began playing "The Star-Spangled Banner" while a hush fell on the crowd. But as soon as the last note was played the crowd was once more in an uproar. Players from each team ran to the center of the field and took their opposing positions. A coin was tossed and the Suffington Sentries took possession of the ball.

The ball was snapped back to number 11,

who caught it, then threw it for a fifteen-yard gain.

"Eddie's the quarterback," explained Pam. Hilary made an entry into her notebook:

> *Eddie Stoner #11*
> *quarterback (ask him what a*
> *quarterback does.)*

Hilary watched the game closely as the Sentries pushed the other team back down the field. It was easy to see why the Suffington team was one of the best in the state. It was also easy to see why Eddie Stoner was the captain of the team. His arm was strong and he seemed to be able to throw the ball anywhere. Hilary thought to herself, he probably wrestles with cows or pigs or something like that to build up his muscles. But she couldn't help admiring him for his athletic ability.

The halftime show was a glitter of band instruments and silver-costumed majorettes twirling fire batons. The band played a song that had the Suffington audience clapping their hands and stomping their feet. Hilary had to admit to herself that the band had a certain sense of excitement.

As the game began to draw to a close with the Sentries ahead by 23 points, Hilary began to feel a little nervous. What would she say to

Eddie after the game? How would she introduce herself? What if he just stared at her like she was weird? she wondered.

With just five minutes left in the game, Hilary whispered to her friends, "Here goes nothing. I'll meet you in the parking lot. Okay?"

"We'll be in the gym," said Bonnie Jean. "I forgot to tell you. There's always a dance after a home game. Dad said we could stay for half an hour."

"Okay. I'll see you there," said Hilary. She began climbing down the bleachers. On the ground at last, she headed for the spot where the Suffington team would leave the football field to return to the school locker room. She reached the edge of the field right as the horn sounded signaling the end of the game. The crowd of spectators began to surge toward the parking lot and school.

Hilary waited, rubbing her nose occasionally to keep it from going numb in the cold night air. She peered through the crowd around her, scanning the team members for number 11. At last she saw him and ran toward him. He held his helmet in his hand and his hair was black, glistening with sweat.

"Eddie? Eddie Stoner?" called Hilary. She was surprised to find that her voice sounded higher than usual. She realized with a start that she sounded like she was nine years old.

"Yeah?" Eddie stopped and turned to look at Hilary. "You talking to me?" he asked.

"Yes, I am," she said. Hilary could almost hear her heart beating as she looked into Eddie's face. The girls had been right. He had to be the cutest guy in the whole junior high school . . . maybe even in the whole town. His eyes were ice blue and his hair was jet black. Blue and black, thought Hilary, like shining black birds flying through a blue summer sky, or like a sleek black seal slipping into a blue lake.

"What do you want?" Eddie repeated. "Hey!" he exclaimed upon closer look. "You're the new girl, aren't you?"

"Yes," said Hilary, regaining her confidence. "I'm Hilary Weathervan. I'm doing an article for the sports page of the *Suffington Sentinel* and I wondered if I could interview you about the team. Since you're the captain and the quarterback, I thought you'd be the best person to talk to."

By now Hilary had fallen into step beside Eddie as he walked back toward the school. Other team members stared with curiosity at Hilary. She tried to ignore them and kept talking to Eddie.

"Could we talk for about ten minutes?" Hilary asked. "If I write a good article, then I can get a job on the school newspaper."

"Where are you from?" asked Eddie. "I heard you were from New York."

"I'm from Philadelphia," said Hilary. "I've visited New York a lot. My aunt lives there. But I'm from Philly."

They were almost at the school by now. Eddie stopped at the door and turned to Hilary. He looked down into her eyes. "Tell you what," he said. "I'll meet you in the gym at the dance. I've got to shower first. I'll meet you by the turntable. My friend Karl is playing records tonight. Tell him that I said that he should play anything you want to hear. Okay?" Eddie winked, then disappeared inside the door.

Hilary looked down at her legs to make sure that they hadn't turned into jelly. But covered as they were by red slacks, she couldn't be sure. She walked around to the side of the building, entered, and found her way to the gym. As soon as she walked in, Pam, Bonnie Jean, and Jerry came hurrying over.

"Did you get your interview?" asked Pam. "Did he talk to you?"

Hilary tried to control her voice. "He's meeting me here for the interview," she said. Then she couldn't stop the grin from spreading across her face. "He's so-o-o cute!" she whispered. The other girls giggled and

Hilary found herself giggling along with them in a way that she never had before. It was just too much to think that *she*, Hilary Weathervan from Philadelphia, was attracted to some guy from farmer town, Massachusetts, whom she'd only met once.

Hilary walked over to the turntable to wait for Eddie. She saw the boy who must be Karl. He was playing records and acting as D.J. "Hello, all you super Sentries' supporters," he said in a voice that made everyone laugh. "Tonight I've got tunes for every mood, and I think there's a crazy mood out there tonight where anything can happen. I can feel some hearts opening up out there and I see the twinkle in those eyes."

Hilary looked at Karl from the corner of her eye to make sure that he wasn't talking about her. Suddenly she felt a hand on her shoulder. "May I have this dance?" asked Eddie. His hair was wet from the shower. He smelled like blue soap.

"They're not playing any music," said Hilary.

"Who needs it?" asked Eddie. He grinned and took Hilary's hand, pulling her into the center of the gym floor. "Hey, Karl!" he yelled. "How about some tunes?"

"Coming right up," said Karl. "I've got just the thing." He set the stereo needle on the record's edge. A slow rhythm of guitars poured from the speakers.

Eddie gently placed a hand on Hilary's back, while holding her hand in his other hand. She timidly put her hand against his shoulder and fell into step. They rocked in time to the music and Eddie whispered in her ear, "You know, I noticed you the very first day you came here. You're different from the other girls. I knew when I first saw you that I wanted to get to know you better."

Hilary couldn't think of anything to say. Her mind whirled with impressions of band music, halftime shows, yelling crowds, and a strong arm that threw the football skillfully.

Eddie's crystal blue eyes gazed down at Hilary. A smile touched the corner of his lips. "Did you want to do that interview now?" he asked. "Where's your notebook?"

"I don't know," said Hilary. "I think I lost it on the fifty-yard line."

Four

Dear Mike,

Sorry I haven't written lately. I sprained my wrist and for a while there, I couldn't hold a pen.

Dear Mike,

Sorry I missed your phone call last Friday. I was down in the basement up to my knees in water when the phone rang. The pipes burst and I had to hold them together while Mom went to get a plumber.

Dear Mike,

I've been in the hospital for the past three weeks. Sorry I didn't write, but the doctors told me that I shouldn't because ... .

Hilary sighed and dropped her pen in

midsentence. She leaned back in her chair, thinking, Hmmm. There's just no good way to tell someone that you're falling in love with someone else.

She thought about Mike and how nice their friendship had been. But now he was hundreds of miles away. It was hard to stay close to someone you never even saw . . . someone you talked to on the phone just once a week.

And then, of course, there was Eddie. Hilary's toes curled inside her bedroom slippers as she thought of his wavy black hair, his bright blue eyes, and the way he threw a football. She had feelings for Eddie that she'd never had for Mike. When she was with Eddie, it was as if her heart began to tremble. Her friendship with Mike seemed boring and babyish in comparison.

It seemed like Hilary's life had turned upside down. The last three weeks had been a dream. Eddie Stoner sat with her at lunch every day. Every other girl in the junior high school looked at her when she walked down the hall. Even girls a year older, in the eighth grade, were starting to talk to her and wanting to be her friend. She'd been asked to join the Pep Club and she had invitations to two slumber parties.

This was quite a bit different from life in

Philadelphia where Hilary had been the quiet girl who "went" with Mike Dillow. In the city's huge junior high school, there weren't many students who had known Hilary's name or face, just the people on the newspaper staff.

But here in Suffington, in the small town school where everyone noticed a "new girl," Hilary felt like a different person. Suddenly, she was popular. She was *very* popular, and it was all because of Eddie Stoner, who was *super* popular.

But there was still the problem of what to do with Mike. It was like an impossible math problem: Two boys plus one girl equals confusion. Hilary just couldn't think of a nice way to tell Mike about Eddie, and she didn't want to hurt him. He was, after all, her oldest friend. So, Hilary decided to set the problem aside, until she could think of a good solution. She crumpled up all the letters to Mike which she'd begun, threw them into her wastebasket, then dashed to the phone in the hall as it began to ring.

"Hello," she said into the receiver.

"Hi, Hilary. This is Dan Ellsworth, editor of *The Suffington Sentinel.* Remember me? I just wanted to know how you're coming with that sports article for *The Sentinel.* It's been a couple of weeks and I haven't heard anything from you. Are you still interested in working for the school newspaper?"

"Oh. Hi, Dan," Hilary said. "Sorry I didn't get back to you sooner. I've been busy unpacking and stuff like that. I think I just don't have enough time to work on the paper right now. Maybe next year, okay?" Hilary hoped that if she made her voice sound cheery and friendly, Dan wouldn't be mad at her for not getting in touch with him about the football article she never wrote. Also, she was a little embarrassed. Dan had probably seen her and the team's quarterback having lunch together every day in the cafeteria.

"Well, if you change your mind, we have a new position opening up on the newspaper staff," said Dan. "In two months, right around Christmas, we're starting a column on health problems. The first one is on phobias. You know, that's when someone's *super* afraid of something, like test phobias. Some kids are really afraid to take tests. We thought that this column could help them learn to deal with it."

"Right," said Hilary. "Sounds interesting. I'll let you know if I change my mind. Bye."

"Bye," said Dan.

"It's funny that Dan should mention phobias," Hilary said to herself. "I think I had a Suffington-phobia until I met Eddie." She smiled to herself.

"Who was on the phone?" her mother called

44

cheerfully from her office.

"No one special," replied Hilary.

"In other words, it wasn't Eddie?" her mother laughed.

"Oh, Mom. Give me a break," said Hilary. Hilary wandered into her mother's study where she sat, as usual, reading over pages of statistics.

"Mom," said Hilary. "Can I talk to you for a minute?"

"Of course, Honey," her mom said. "What's on your mind?" She took off her reading glasses to look at Hilary.

"Well," said Hilary, cocking her head to one side. "I was just wondering. How did you break up with dad when you decided that you didn't want to be married anymore? What did you say to him? Did you cry?"

"We both cried," her mom said. She sighed, and a troubled look came into her eyes. "We both wanted to end the marriage," she said. "It wasn't just me. Your father and I knew for several years that our marriage wasn't working out."

"But how did you end it?" asked Hilary. "Did you write him a letter, or did you talk to him?"

Mrs. Weathervan pushed her books and papers to one side of the desk, as she leaned forward on her arms. "I guess it really ended one day when I told him that I was going to pack some things and call a divorce lawyer. Your father and I agreed that it would be best for you to stay with me, since he's a salesman. Remember all the times he spent on the road?" she asked.

Hilary looked worried. Her mom continued, "And mostly, I wanted you very, very much because I love you. You know that, don't you?"

Hilary nodded. She felt her throat become tight with emotion. She had come into her mom's office to get information on how to drop Mike as easily as possible. But instead, she got a peek into her mother's heart. Hilary looked at her mother with new tenderness and respect. "Was it hard?" she asked. "Did it hurt you to break up with Dad?"

"It always hurts," said her mom. "Breaking up, leaving friends, it's always hard. But it's also a sign of growing up to be able to do it without breaking apart. Sometimes we just have to leave someone even if it hurts."

Hilary stood up and walked to her mom's side. As she lay her hand on her mom's arm she said, "You work too hard, Mom. You know that?"

"Yes, I know." Edith Weathervan grinned shyly at her daughter.

"Why don't you put that stuff away and let's go out to the kitchen for a bedtime snack,"

Hilary suggested. She smiled. She really did love her mom.

"Okay," her mom said. "Why not?"

Hilary spread peanut butter on crackers, then passed them to her mom who crowned them with a bit of raspberry jam. They munched crackers and drank milk in the kitchen's warm white light.

"Mom, what should I do about Mike?" asked Hilary. "I know he'll feel awful if I tell him about Eddie. Mike was planning to come up for Thanksgiving, but I don't want him to come anymore."

"It's usually best to be direct and honest," said her mom. "He'll hurt for a while. But if you keep lying to him, he'll know something's wrong, then he won't have the opportunity to get over it, and he'll hurt for a lot longer." She sighed. "It's hard on you, too. I know. It hurts to leave someone you used to care for. But, Hilary, my dear daughter, it's easier to deal with problems than it is to ignore them and pretend that they're not there," she said, smiling.

"Then, I guess I'll deal with it," said Hilary. "Good night, Mom. Thanks."

"Good night, Honey."

Hilary went to her room. She sat at her desk once again with a sheet of paper before her. She began to write:

Dear Mike,

There's something that I need to tell you. I don't want to hurt your feelings, but you've been my good friend for a long time and I don't want to lie to you.

I have a boyfriend in Suffington. His name is Eddie Stoner and we're practically going steady . . .

Five

HILARY sat at the living room window and watched the snow fall. The November evening outside was cold, casting a bluish light over the sparkling white landscape. Hilary listened closely for the sound which would signal the arrival of Eddie and a dozen more kids from school. At last it came. The tingle of jingle bells and the steady clop-clop of a horse's hooves shattered the evening's quietness and began growing louder. At last, Hilary saw the hay wagon pull up in front of her house. Through the falling snow she caught glimpses of brightly colored mittens, scarves, and woolen caps.

"Hey, Cinderella!" came Eddie's familiar voice. "Come on! Your coach is waiting!"

"Bye, Mom," called Hilary. She pulled on her heavy jacket and gloves and ran outside into the swirling white flakes. The cold air stung her cheeks. Eddie jumped down from the wagon and helped Hilary up. She didn't need the help, but it was nice to have someone pay attention to her. "Hi, Eddie," she said, once again noticing that her voice seemed to be higher than usual. It was strange how being around Eddie made her feel.

"Hey, Hilary!" called Jerry.

"Hi, Hilary!" came Bonnie Jean's voice, muffled through a scarf.

"Hi!" yelled Pam from the back of the wagon.

"Hi, Hilary," said Dan Ellsworth quietly. He was sitting next to Michelle Deason.

Voices from behind scarves and ski masks greeted Hilary. She waved to everyone, then snuggled down into the hay, which was more scratchy than warm. A man bundled up in an overcoat and a hat with earflaps sat in the driver's seat with a blanket over his knees. "Hello there, young lady," he said. Hilary peered through the dancing snowflakes to see the friendly face of Mr. Kite.

"Is this one of your farm horses?" asked Hilary.

"Sure is," said Mr. Kite. "Her name's Rosie. She doesn't work anymore, though. Too old for that. She's out to pasture these days, living the good life and pulling a wagonload of kids every once in awhile." Mr. Kite shook the bell-covered reins. "Giddap!" he yelled.

Rosie obligingly began with a slow walk into

the drift-covered road. Mr. Kite shook the reins again, and Rosie broke into a heavy trot. With each step, the bells shivered and tinkled.

Bruce McGee, the seventh grade class clown, took a handful of straw and stuck it under his cap. "Look!" he cried to the group. "I'm a scarecrow!"

"You don't need straw under your hat to prove that!" came Eddie's reply.

"Was that an insult? This means war!" laughed Bruce. He grabbed the straw from under his cap and tossed it at Eddie. The straw stung Eddie's ear and fell to his lap. Eddie picked up a handful and threw it back at Bruce, but some of it fell on Angie Vincent. "Hey," she yelled. "Watch where you throw that stuff!" She scooped an armful of straw against her chest, then heaved it out in Eddie's direction. Suddenly, straw was flying in every direction. Everyone laughed and shrieked, which also meant that everyone ended up with a little straw in their mouths. From the frenzy of falling snow and flying straw came exclamations and giggles:

"Ow! Watch it, you big jerk!"

"No! No! I've got my contacts in!"

"That'll teach you! Ha! Ha! Ha!"

"Timmy, no! I mean it! Oh!"

"Eeee-eee-ee!" Hilary recognized the shriek as Jerry Dapple's. Hilary felt prickly with bits

51

of straw stuck to her hair and jacket. Some of it slipped from her head, tickling her neck.

"You look like a porcupine," Eddie teased her.

"Thanks a lot," said Hilary, laughing. "You don't exactly look like Robert Redford yourself."

"You're darn right, I don't," Eddie said. "I look a lot better!" He grinned at her, and although he was joking, Hilary had to agree. Not many boys could look cuter than Eddie did right then, his blue eyes winking in the snow as falling flakes touched his eyelashes.

The group settled down as Rosie calmly pulled the hay wagon over paved roads until she reached the edge of town.

"You look pretty tonight," Eddie whispered into Hilary's ear. "You look like one of those city girls I see in magazines."

"What's so great about city girls?" asked Hilary. "I didn't think we were any different from other kinds of girls."

"I don't know," said Eddie. "You just seem more grown-up, or something. You've been more places than I have. I hope I get out of this town someday."

"Why?" asked Hilary.

"It's too small. I know everyone and everyone knows me, my parents, and my brothers. I'd like to go somewhere else where no one knows me."

"I know what you mean," said Hilary. "I didn't like it when I first moved here, but it's turning out to be a lot of fun, even though no one knows me."

"I know you," said Eddie. "I know that you have neat clothes, and you like soft pretzels with mustard, and you like to write, and your middle name is Anna. I know that you like to dance, and you think that *Huckleberry Finn* is the best book you ever read. Also, your favorite color is blue, right?"

"Right," said Hilary, gazing into Eddie's eyes.

Michelle Deason leaned over and whispered into Hilary's ear, "I'm having a party on the eighteenth. That's two weeks away. It's for all the football players and their girl friends. Want to come?"

"Sure," said Hilary. "I'll be there. Thanks." It was neat to be thought of as "Eddie's girl friend." It made Hilary feel like she belonged. Besides that, Hilary never thought she'd have a boyfriend as cute and popular as Eddie. It must mean that *she* was cute and popular, too.

Suddenly, the wagon tilted at a crazy angle. Girls, boys, and straw began to slide over the side and fall to the ground.

"Whoah, there!" yelled Mr. Kite. "Whoah, girl!" Rosie snorted and pranced.

"What is it, Mr. Kite? What happened?" asked Eddie, picking himself up from the snow and pulling Hilary out of the drift that she'd tumbled into.

Mr. Kite jumped down from the driver's seat. He looked back at the wagon and said, "Darn it! It's the rear wheel. It broke."

Hilary looked at the left rear wheel of the wagon and discovered that the wooden spokes had broken and part of the rim had collapsed. "Oh, no!" she said. "What are we going to do?"

"I've got hot cider here in a thermos," said Mr. Kite, "so, we won't freeze. But we're going to need a new wheel." He stood in the snow, thoughtfully scratching his chin. "Amos Perdy lives right down the road here," he said. One of you kids will have to go to Mr. Purdy's for help." He looked at the group of kids as they shook snow out of their coat sleeves and brushed their knees. "Any volunteers?"

"I'll go," Eddie piped up immediately. "I know Mr. Perdy pretty well. I mow his yard in the summer, so I know where his house is. You want to come, Hilary?"

"I don't know," said Hilary. The thought of walking out into the dark, snowy night into a countryside that she didn't know, was a little frightening. "How far away is it? Are you sure you know where you're going?" she asked.

"I've been there a million times," said Eddie. "It's not far. Come on. It'll be fun."

"Okay," said Hilary hesitantly. "If you say so."

"Great! We'll both go," Eddie told Mr. Kite.

"We're not going to freeze, are we?" asked Angie with tears in her eyes.

"Of course not," said Mr. Kite consolingly. "Eddie here is in good shape. He'll make it to Perdy's. Now you be careful, little lady," he said to Hilary.

"I will," Hilary said. She turned and joined Eddie as he began trudging down the snow-covered road. She heard the voices of her schoolmates fade into the night. Soon the only sound to be heard was the crunch-crunch of snow beneath her feet and Eddie's. Unrelenting, the snow continued to fall in swirls and bursts. Through the snow, Hilary caught glimpses of the bare, skeleton-handed branches of the trees that grew beside the road. Suddenly, she felt a warm, mittened hand in hers as she walked along. She looked at Eddie and saw that he was smiling at her. "Don't be afraid," he said. "I'm here. I'll take care of you."

Hilary felt relieved. Feelings crowded her head and her heart. It was like she had a snowstorm of emotions swirling inside her. With the storm blowing around them, Eddie stopped in the middle of the road. He took Hilary's other hand in his and stood facing her. She stood there looking back at Eddie and wondering what he wanted. At last she said, "Eddie, we can't stand here all night. My toes are freezing."

Eddie laughed. "Yes, we can," he said. "We'll stand here all night if we have to."

"What are you talking about?" asked Hilary.

"We're talking about going steady," said Eddie. "I'm going to make you stand here with me all night until you say you'll go steady with me."

"What?" she asked. Hilary couldn't believe what she was hearing. Was she really standing in the middle of a country road with the captain of the Suffington football team asking her to go steady with him? Not only that, but he had the bluest eyes in the world and he knew that she loved to dance. He knew about a million other things, too. It all seemed to be too good to be true.

"Yes," said Hilary. "I'll go steady with you. I'd like that very much." Suddenly shy, she pulled her hands away and stuck them in her pockets.

"What's the matter?" asked Eddie. "Are you embarrassed to be my girl friend?"

"Oh, it's not that," Hilary hastened to say. "It's just . . . it's just . . . well . . . I don't know.

I feel funny. That's all."

"I feel funny, too," said Eddie. "I kind of like it though, don't you?"

Hilary nodded. She couldn't trust her voice right now. She hoped that Eddie could see her nod through the darkness and the snow. Even if he didn't, she knew that he would know that she was happy to be his girl friend. What girl wouldn't be?

Eddie hooked his arm through Hilary's and they began trudging once more down the glistening country road. The snow continued to fall, sparkling and soft as a dream.

Six

A week had passed since the night of the
hayride. Eddie had been the hero of the
evening, getting the spare wheel from Mr.
Perdy, then carrying it back to the broken hay
wagon. The kids and Mr. Kite cheered when
they saw him coming. Hilary walked beside
him, proud to be his steady girl friend.
Everything that had to do with Eddie was
perfect.

* * * * *

"But Mom," Hilary complained. "She's
driving me nuts. She really is. I can't even
open the curtains on my window without
seeing her hiding up there, watching me. It's
really creepy. I have to always make sure my
blinds are closed, so she can't see in."

"Why don't you go over and introduce
yourself?" asked Hilary's mom. "I'm sure Mrs.
Suffington is probably a very nice, lonely

58

lady. She'd probably like the company."

Wasn't it just like her mom to say something like that? thought Hilary. Here was her own mom ready to sacrifice her daughter to a crazy old lady with no teeth and no hair.

"Why don't you go over and talk to Mrs. Suffington?" she asked. "Explain to her that it bothers you to have her looking in your window. I'm sure she'd be very happy to listen to you."

"Yeah, right," Hilary said sarcastically. "She'll just tie me up and throw me in her spidery old basement, or something like that."

"Oh, Hilary," her mom said. "You're exaggerating. Honey, if you're really serious about being a writer, you're going to have to learn how to investigate things . . . follow through on stories. Just pretend that you've been given an assignment to write about Mrs. Suffington. Pretend that you have to interview her, and if you do good work, you'll be given a job as head of the *New York Times*."

"I'd rather write for *Mad Magazine*," said Hilary.

"Well then, pretend you'll be given the editorship of *Mad Magazine*," said Mrs. Weathervan. "Good heavens! You're picky."

"Okay. I'll do it," said Hilary. "I'll go over there. But, if anything happens to me, remember, it's your fault!"

Edith Weathervan just shook her head and smiled while Hilary pulled on her jacket and gloves.

"Okay, Mom," Hilary said as she walked out the door. "Just remember that you're the one who made me move to this weird town with its weird people. I never had to go and talk to baldheaded little old ladies when we lived in Philly."

Hilary closed the door behind her and walked through the melting snow to the side of her house. Seven days of sunshine had melted the snow and turned it into dirty patches of ice and black mud.

"What am I going to say to her?" Hilary asked herself as she opened the back gate and crossed into Mrs. Suffington's backyard. As she drew further away from her own home, she noticed that even though it was the middle of the afternoon, the blinds were drawn at every single window in the gray-shingled house. What kind of person would want to live all closed up in a house? It would be kind of like living in a tomb, Hilary imagined.

The front porch sagged and creaked under her weight. Hilary stepped over a broken board, then knocked on the door. She listened for noises, but heard none. She knocked again, then stood silently, feeling her heart begin to beat a faster rhythm. From somewhere above her she heard movement. Slowly, very slowly, the inside stairs began to creak from the second floor down to the first. One after another, the footsteps grew closer. A gnarled hand pushed aside the dusty drape at the door's window. A red-rimmed eye peered out at Hilary.

"Why, she's no taller than I am!" was Hilary's first reaction. "Oh, good. She has hair," was Hilary's second.

The doorknob turned and slowly the door was pulled open. A soft face under a fluff of white hair looked out. "What do you want?" Mrs. Suffington asked. Her voice shook with age. Or was it fear? Hilary wasn't sure which.

"Hello, Mrs. Suffington. I'm your neighbor, Hilary Weathervan. I live in the white house behind you. I just moved here a few months ago from Philadelphia. I thought I'd come over and introduce myself. Also, I wanted to talk to you about something."

"Are there others with you?" asked Mrs. Suffington. Her voice creaked and shook. "Are those kids hiding behind the house again?"

Hilary looked puzzled. "No, ma'am," she said. "I came alone."

"Well, come on in, then. But hurry up. I don't like to leave my door open like this. Hurry!" Mrs. Suffington snapped.

Hilary pushed the door wider and slipped

inside the house. A musty smell of old furniture and still air hit her nose immediately.

"Come in here," said Mrs. Suffington. She crept along with her bent back into the parlor. "Sit down," she said.

Hilary sat on a hard red velvet sofa. At least, it used to be red. Now it was a dark reddish-brown. It looked as if it could be a hundred years old. Around her on the walls were pictures in gilt frames. Faces of fat-cheeked women, their hair in buns, looked down at her. Men with handlebar moustaches gazed directly in front of themselves. There were photos everywhere.

"That's Uriah," said Mrs. Suffington. She pointed to a yellowing photo of a man standing beside a bicycle. She lifted it from the table and handed it to Hilary. "Now, there's a man for you," she said. "He treated me like a queen." She sighed, lost in memory.

Somehow the fear of being tied up and thrown in the basement left Hilary's thoughts completely. This woman could hardly walk, much less tie up a healthy young girl like a calf in a rodeo. But, she could always offer me a drink with poison in it, thought Hilary.

"Would you like some tea?" asked Mrs. Suffington. "I just made a fresh pot. It's rose hips." Before Hilary could say a word, Mrs. Suffington turned and slowly made her way over to the china cabinet in the dining room. She opened the glass door and gingerly removed a fragile-looking cup and saucer. She turned and walked toward Hilary, holding the cup and saucer with both hands. She carefully placed the cup and saucer in front of Hilary. After sitting down she picked up the pot on the table before her and poured Hilary a cup of steaming tea. A smell of warm flowers drifted into Hilary's nostrils. Oh well, Hilary said to herself after a sip. If it's poison, at least it tastes good. Hilary set her cup on the table. Mrs. Suffington poured herself a cup and Hilary noticed how badly the old woman's hands were shaking. Once again, she had the feeling that the trembling was due to age and also to fear. But what was she afraid of? Surely, it couldn't be Hilary. How could anyone be afraid of a thirteen-year-old girl who loved to write and dance?

"Uriah's been dead for twenty-two years now," said Mrs. Suffington. "I'm just glad he's not here to see what's happened to the younger generation. Kids today have no respect. They're a bunch of hooligans."

"I'm not a hooligan," said Hilary.

For the very first time, Mrs. Suffington smiled. The creases at the edges of her eyes deepened and her lips crimped upward. Hilary was relieved to see that she had teeth after all, even if they were fake and tea-stained. "I'm very glad to hear that you're not a hooligan, dear," said Mrs. Suffington. She reached out to pat the back of Hilary's hand. Mrs. Suffington's hand was spotted with brown patches, and blue veins stuck up like spiderwebs. But her hand was soft and gentle like a kitten's paw. "I don't get out much anymore," said Mrs. Suffington.

"Why not?" asked Hilary. "Why don't you ever come out of your house?"

"It's all the people out there," said Mrs. Suffington. "They're a bunch of hooligans."

She's afraid, Hilary thought, with a shock. She's afraid to leave the house because she thinks everyone's out to get her. How awful! She stays in here shut up and alone all the time. "Are you afraid of *everyone*?" asked Hilary.

"Of course," said Mrs. Suffington. "Why shouldn't I be, what with kids and everyone being the way they are today. They're all hooligans! That's what they are!"

"When was the last time you were out of the house?" asked Hilary.

"Oh, let's see. I think it was, yes, it must have been 19 and 69. Yes, I believe I went to see my sister-in-law Beverley on her sixty-fifth birthday back in Pittsburgh in 1969. I took a bus there and you wouldn't believe the hooligans that were on that bus. Even the bus driver was a rascal. He had hair down to his shoulders. It looked like a mop."

"It's been over fifteen years since you've been out of the house?" asked Hilary. "That's before I was even born! Don't you get lonely?"

"The grocery-boy comes every week," the white-haired lady informed Hilary. "And the plumber came a few years back. I had a leak in the upstairs toilet."

"But don't you want to get outside and see what's going on?" asked Hilary. "Don't you wonder about all the new people in town that you've never met? I'll bet lots of new people have moved here in the last twenty years."

"I'm sure they have," said Mrs. Suffington. "And I know what they all are, too."

"Hooligans?" asked Hilary.

"Now you're catching on," said Mrs. Suffington, winking a tired eye.

"Would you come outside if I took you?" asked Hilary. "We could go some place together, and I wouldn't let any hooligans get you, I promise."

"You're a good girl," Mrs. Suffington said kindly. "But I don't want to go out there, and that's that." Her lips and hands began to tremble violently, and Hilary could see that she was becoming upset at the very thought of leaving the house.

"That's okay," said Hilary. "Let's not talk about it anymore. Why don't you tell me about your husband, Uriah. Wasn't it his great grandfather who founded Suffington?"

* * * * *

The afternoon wore on as Hilary listened to tales of a brave man named Zachary Suffington. He was the Suffington who had blazed a trail through a wilderness of trees and came at last upon a little spot in Massachusetts. This spot, he felt, was lovely enough to bear his name and to become a home to his family. Once there, he built a cabin. Then he sent for his neighbors and wife, Sarah, back in his old hometown. It took them weeks to find their way to the little cabin in the woods. When they got there the men sawed timber for more cabins. The women dug the earth to plant vegetable gardens beside their new homes. Their children played in a nearby stream and grew up in the town that came to be known as Suffington.

"More tea, dear?" Mrs. Suffington asked.

"Yes, thank you," said Hilary. "That's okay. I'll pour it." She lifted the china pot and poured a cup for herself and one for the reminiscing, pink-faced lady beside her.

Twenty years of loneliness came bubbling

from Mrs. Suffington's mouth. All the conversations she'd never had, and all the stories she'd never shared, were shared with Hilary. Many of the stories were about how strong and wonderful her husband, Uriah, had been.

"What time is it?" Hilary suddenly asked, jumping up from the couch. She ran to the window and lifted a curtain. A shower of dust fell on her head, causing her to sneeze. "Oh, my!" she said. "It's late. It's after dinnertime. Mom will be worried. I'd better go."

"But you just got here," said Mrs. Suffington.

"The sun's gone down. Don't worry. I'll be back," said Hilary. "If you won't come out then I guess I'll just have to come in, won't I? I'll be back tomorrow afternoon, okay?"

The old woman and the young woman looked at each other and smiled. The bright hazel eyes and the red-rimmed eyes met in the discovery of newfound friendship and understanding. Hilary leaned forward and planted a kiss on the withered cheek. "Bye," she said. "I'll be back." Then she opened the front door and disappeared into the evening. The door behind her closed immediately as Mrs. Suffington began, once again, to peep from behind the curtain.

It must be awful to be so afraid to be with

people, Hilary thought to herself as she ran back to her home. Her mother had kept her dinner warm, and Hilary ate it quickly, then went upstairs to her room.

She sat at her desk, and instead of making sure that the blinds were tightly shut like she usually did, she pulled the cord and let the blind roll, flapping up to the top of the window. Hilary pulled her lamp closer so that she would be bathed in its golden light. With the blind open and the bright light, Hilary could easily be seen from a distance. She pushed her face closer to her window and squinted into the dark night. Then she raised her hand and gave a cheerful wave. She wasn't sure, but she thought she saw a movement at the second-floor window of the gray-shingled house. Was it a hand waving in return? she wondered.

Hilary bowed her head over the sheet of notepaper before her and began to write:

A Lonely Heart

When I'm alone inside my heart,
I yell and scream to let you know
that I'm alone and I'm afraid.
I'm too afraid to let fear go.

With doors and hearts
locked tight with keys . . .

Hilary couldn't think of anything to rhyme with the word "keys" except for the word "cheese." The idea of eating cheese didn't fit into the poem, so she pushed the poem aside, waved at Mrs. Suffington again, and pulled another piece of paper into the light before her. She would finish the poem at another time when she felt more like it. Right now thoughts of Eddie chased away thoughts of Mrs. Suffington. This was no time to be writing about lonely hearts. She began to write:

EDDIE
+
HILARY

Eddie Loves Hilary Loves Eddie

Steady Eddie

Hilary Weathervan + Eddie Stoner

Weatherstone Stonevan Hilary Stoner

Seven

JERRY met Hilary beside her locker between second and third periods. "Are you and Eddie going to Michelle Deason's party this Saturday?" she asked.

"Yeah," said Hilary. "Are you?"

"Not unless I start dating a football player real fast," laughed Jerry. "Michelle's just having it for all the Junior Varsity players and their girl friends. She's got this thing about jocks."

"I wish you were going to be there," said Hilary. "It's going to be mostly eighth graders and I won't know anyone."

"You'll do fine," said Jerry. "Anyway, you'll be with Eddie. He'll take care of you."

Hilary thought about it. That was true. When she was with Eddie, everyone came up and talked to her. She really didn't have to think of much to say because Eddie always had a joke or comment. He could make everyone laugh. Everyone thought he was great. He introduced her to people and took her places, so she never had to do those things alone. It would have been a lot scarier for her as the "new girl" in town if she didn't have Eddie by her side. He took care of her and made her feel very special, like a china doll. It was nice to know that someone cared.

That day after school, Eddie walked Hilary home. He carried her books for her. "What are you going to wear to the party this Saturday?" he asked. "I'd like you to wear something real special, like a dress seen in a fashion magazine."

"Sure," said Hilary. "I can wear that if you want me to. I have a really nice dress that Mom got for me in Boston last year. It's real cute."

"Great!" said Eddie. "I know you'll look super. The other girls always look boring compared to you. You know, every other guy on the team would give anything to go out with you," Eddie said. "But I got you first." He grinned.

"Oh, Eddie," said Hilary. She was embarrassed. Eddie was always saying things like that. Sometimes she felt a little like a prize in a bingo game. "Here we are," she said. They stopped in front of Hilary's house and Eddie handed her her books. "I'll see you at school tomorrow," he said. "Bye."

Hilary watched as Eddie strolled down the sidewalk and disappeared around the corner. He looked extra strong when he was wearing his letter jacket. The sleeves were soft white leather and the rest of it was pine green. Hilary climbed the porch steps and went into her house. She heard a sound coming from the kitchen. "Mom, is that you?" she called.

"Yes, Hilary," came the reply. "I left work early today. I decided that I'd cook us a regular dinner tonight, no carry-out food. How does that sound?"

"What's the occasion, Mom?" asked Hilary. "Is it someone's birthday?"

"No, Hon. I just thought that maybe I've been working too hard and I should spend a little more time being a mom," Hilary's mom said. She pulled a tin of applesauce muffins from the oven. "Mmmm," she said, sniffing. "These smell wonderful. Want one?"

"Before the rest of the dinner is done?" asked Hilary.

"Sure," said her mom. "We'll have a preview."

Hilary spread butter on the hot muffin. She took a bite and steam burst out from the yellow cake. "Mmmm, good," Hilary said. Then she cocked her head to one side and asked, "Mom, why do you work so hard? I mean, why do you bring papers and stuff home from work and why is your job so important to you? Is it just the money?"

"No," her mom said. "The money's nice, I must admit." She smiled. "But actually, I just like to work. It's as simple as that. If I wasn't working, I'd probably be doing something else, like worrying about how long my fingernails are, you know, important stuff like that."

"Come on, Mom," said Hilary. "I'm serious."

"So am I!" exclaimed Mrs. Weathervan. "What I mean is, work is important to me. When I work hard I discover just what I'm capable of doing. And I guess what's so exciting is that I'm finding that I'm capable of doing a lot. I never used to think I could hold down a job as a market analyst, but I can. And to tell you the truth, I'm one of the best in the company. It's a good feeling."

"Work is a good feeling?" asked Hilary doubtfully. "Are you cracking up, Mom?" she asked jokingly.

"It's a great feeling, Honey," she said. "You'll discover that one of these days. Speaking of work, how's your writing coming? Have you written the great American novel, yet?"

"Give me a break, Mom," said Hilary. "No, I haven't been doing too much writing lately. I've been too busy at school."

"You mean with Eddie?" asked her mom.

"Yeah. I guess so," Hilary said, looking a little sheepish. "I've been staying after school to watch Eddie work out with the basketball team. He's not on the team, but he wants to stay in shape for football, so he works out with them. He's really serious about playing on a college team when he graduates from high school. You should see him play sometime. He's really good."

"So are you," said her mom.

"Are you kidding?" exclaimed Hilary. "I couldn't throw a football if you paid me!"

"That's not what I mean," she said. "I mean, you're a very good writer. You should keep up with it, work at it."

"Can I have another muffin, Mom?" asked Hilary. "They're great!" Hilary had learned that at times like these, when work or grades were becoming the topic of discussion, it was often best to change the subject. The last thing she wanted to talk about right now was her writing. She hadn't been doing much of it lately, but, Hilary told herself, writers have to take a rest every now and then. She had to decide her priorities. Surely, making friends and having a boyfriend like Eddie were more important than writing poems about lonely hearts and stuff like that.

Mrs. Weathervan opened the oven door and

pulled out a roasting pan. She lifted the lid and the aroma of chicken permeated the kitchen. "Yum!" she said. "Dinner's ready."

* * * * *

The week slipped by and Saturday seemed to come in the wink of an eye. Hilary was excited about Michelle's party, as was every other girl who had been invited. Hilary pulled the green dress she planned to wear from its hanger. It's skirt was a mini so she wore a pair of white tights. It was perfect for the football player party since the school colors were green and white.

Hilary used styling mousse on her short blonde hair. She brushed the sides straight back, then she made waves on the top. It looked really neat. No one in Suffington wears their hair like this. Hilary thought it looked kind of like the hairstyle of motorcycle guys in old movies. Eddie would love it.

When 7:30 came, Eddie knocked at the front door. First, Hilary waved to Mrs. Suffington from her bedroom window. Then she turned around so that the older woman could see how pretty she looked. Then she ran down the stairs just as her mother opened the front door. "You kids have a good time," she said. "Remember Eddie, I want Hilary home by 10:30. Okay? Will you do that?"

"Sure thing, Mrs. Weathervan," said Eddie. He took Hilary by the elbow and led her down the porch steps. They got into the car where his older brother was waiting to drive them to Michelle's. "You look great," said Eddie enthusiastically. "You look like you just stepped out of a fashion magazine. Have you ever thought about becoming a model?" His blue eyes flashed. Hilary felt safe and happy sitting next to him in the car's backseat.

The party at Michelle's was in full swing when they got there. Kids stood around a table helping themselves to punch. Others were dancing. Angie Vincent was sitting on the floor looking through the record collection. There were quite a few eighth-graders there, and among them were strange faces that Hilary had never seen before. "Hi, Hilary," said Michelle. "Glad you could make it. I've got somebody for you to meet. She's out in the kitchen right now getting some potato chips. She's my cousin, Mimi, from New York. She's staying with us for the next three months while her parents are in Europe. I thought you'd like another city girl to talk to. I know how you miss Philadelphia. Or you used to, anyway," she said, winking at Eddie. Eddie grinned and squeezed Hilary's hand.

"Wow!" Hilary said to herself, "Another new

girl from the city!" That was great. Now she would have someone to talk to about museums, subways, art shows, concerts, fashions, and stuff like that. Hilary like Jerry, Pam, Bonnie Jean, and some of the other girls, but they seemed to be different from her. She missed the company of a city person. Where was this Mimi?

"Let's dance," said Eddie, as a slow song began to play. Hilary and Eddie had danced together about a thousand times by now. She knew just how he was going to move, and she could follow him perfectly. As her cheek rested against his shoulder, Hilary listened dreamily to the soft, lilting music. Hilary watched the other couples rocking back and forth around her.

As she looked, she suddenly came face to face with a girl she'd never seen before. She couldn't be one of the eighth graders because surely Hilary would have noticed *this* girl before. Her hair was jet black, and very short. It was brushed straight back on the sides, and the top was in little waves. She was wearing a bright red miniskirt with clear plastic boots. So this was Mimi! She was dancing with one of the other football players. Hilary smiled at her. It was great! At last there was another city girl in Suffington. The song ended and Michelle came rushing over. She grabbed

Mimi and pulled her over to Hilary and Eddie. "This is Mimi," she announced. "She's from New York!"

"Hi," said Hilary. "I just moved here a few months ago from Philly. Ever been there?"

"No," said Mimi. "I go for the larger cities. New York keeps me pretty busy."

"Wow!" said Eddie. "New York is pretty huge, isn't it? Suffington must seem like a real cow town to you, doesn't it?" he asked, grinning.

"Oh, it's hard to tell," said Mimi. She smiled. She had dimples. "I've only been here a few days," she said. "I have to admit that some of the boys here are real cute." She looked straight into Eddie's blue eyes.

Suddenly, Hilary didn't feel so good. She felt like waves of electricity were passing back and forth between Eddie and Mimi. For once, she wasn't the "new girl" in the crowd and Mimi made her feel small-townish. She was from New York City and Hilary was only from Philadelphia. In comparison, Philly wasn't such a great city. Hilary noticed that Mimi's ears were triple-pierced. "Come on, Eddie," Hilary said. "Let's get some punch. I'm kind of thirsty."

"You go ahead," said Eddie. "I'm not thirsty." Hilary pulled away from him and stared at him questioningly. Eddie leaned down and whispered in her ear. "I'm just trying to be friendly. You know what it's like to be alone and new. I just want to introduce her to a few people and make her feel at home. I'll catch you a little later."

Hilary walked away and headed for the punch table. She was a little hesitant without Eddie by her side, walking through this crowd of people. Suddenly, she felt odd and alone. She poured herself a cup of punch and stood, watching the scene around her.

A fast dance began blaring from the stereo. Everyone rushed out to the middle of the floor and began hopping and dancing. Eddie and Mimi danced together. They talked nonstop and Mimi kept smiling, her dimples flashing. She cupped her hand to her mouth and whispered something into Eddie's ear that made him throw back his head with laughter. Hilary sipped her punch, then turned away, trying not to stare. She didn't want anyone to know how uncomfortable she felt. Also, she didn't want anyone to think that she was jealous. But she was.

The song ended. Hilary watched Eddie from the corner of her eye, waiting to see if he was going to join her at the punch table. He turned to look at Hilary and raised one finger as if to say that he'd be over in a minute. Then another song started and Mimi began to walk away, but Eddie said something to her and she turned around and began to dance with him again. Hilary felt as if her stomach had dropped into her shoes.

What was happening? she wondered. She'd come to this party with a date, and suddenly, she was standing alone in a corner feeling like she'd crashed the party.

She walked back into the kitchen so that she wouldn't be tempted to stand and stare at Eddie and Mimi. No one was in the kitchen. Everyone was out in the other room dancing. Hilary stood alone. She listened to the sounds of music and conversation coming from the next room.

At last the song ended and a slow song began. She felt a tremor in her heart. A slow song always meant that she could stand close to Eddie with her cheek resting softly against him, while he whispered into her ear about how nice she looked. She waited expectantly for the sounds of footsteps coming into the kitchen, footsteps that meant that Eddie was coming to ask her to dance. She waited and waited. Slow music kept playing and Hilary could only imagine that Eddie and Mimi were still dancing. But, maybe Eddie was looking for her and couldn't find her. She had said that she would be by the punch table. Maybe he was over there looking for her.

Hilary walked back into the next room. Eddie was holding Mimi in his arms and he was whispering something in her ear. Mimi dimpled and blushed. Was Eddie telling her how beautiful she was? Hilary wondered. Was he telling her that she was different from all the other girls at the party? Confusion swept through Hilary like an ocean wave. It crushed her. What was happening? Her world seemed to be collapsing. Was it okay for a steady boyfriend to dance with someone else? But, weren't three dances in a row too many?

It became four dances, as another song began to play. Judd Grolling, the tight end on the football team, came into the kitchen for a bottle opener. "What are you doing in here?" he asked.

"O-oh," Hilary stammered. "I just wanted a glass of water." Her voice shook.

Judd looked at her curiously. Then he stuck his neck out the kitchen door, peering into the crowd of dancers. "Oh, I see," he said. "Eddie's found himself another city girl."

"What do you mean?" asked Hilary.

"Nothing. Nothing at all," said Judd. "Want to dance? You look really nice tonight."

Hilary didn't want to dance with Judd. She'd never danced with anyone in Suffington before, except for Eddie. But she didn't want to stand alone in the kitchen all night like a

wallflower, either. So she said, "Yes." She
followed Judd into the other room. Was it her
imagination or was everyone looking at her?
she wondered. She tried to smile as she
danced with Judd. She tried to pretend that
everything was okay, and that she was having
a good time. She wouldn't let anyone know
that inside her heart was breaking. She
wouldn't let them know that a smile was
masking how she felt on the inside. She tried
to tell herself that she was overreacting and
that Eddie was just being friendly to a girl who
was new in town. She tried to tell herself that
everything was okay, but deep down, she knew
that it wasn't. Eddie didn't make a move to
come over and be with her for the rest of the
evening.

At last it was a quarter after ten and Hilary
had to force herself to go to Eddie. She smiled
broadly as she said, "Sorry, Eddie. But it's
getting late and I have to go home."

"Oh! Did you two come together?" asked
Mimi.

"Yeah," said Eddie. "This is my friend
Hilary. I gave her a lift to the party."

Hilary couldn't believe what she was
hearing. Eddie was acting so differently. He
wasn't admitting to Mimi that she, Hilary
Weathervan, was in fact his steady girl friend.

Eddie's brother drove up in front of

Michelle's house and honked. Eddie and Hilary pulled on their jackets and walked out the front door. "What's going on, Eddie?" asked Hilary. "What's happening? You didn't talk to me all night!"

"There's something I've been meaning to tell you, Hilary," Eddie said, with a grim look on his face. Hilary held her breath as she waited for his words. "I think we've been seeing too much of each other," said Eddie. "I think we need to start dating other people. You need to get out and meet some new people."

"But I don't want to meet new people," said Hilary. Eddie opened the car door and they climbed into the backseat. "I'm happy with you," she whispered in a trembling voice, not wanting Eddie's brother to hear.

They drove in silence back to Hilary's house. At least there was silence on the outside. On the inside Hilary was screaming, "Don't leave me! Don't leave me, Eddie! I love you!"

Eddie's brother pulled up to the curb before Hilary's house. Eddie got out and opened the door. He waited for Hilary to climb out. He didn't touch her elbow or help her up the sidewalk like he usually did.

"Will you call me tomorrow?" asked Hilary at her front door. She trembled at the fear of losing Eddie. "Are we still going to the movies?"

"No," said Eddie. "I think we better cool it for a while. You know you can go out with lots of guys. Judd Grolling asked me tonight if I'd mind if he asked you out."

"What did you say?" asked Hilary in a barely audible voice.

"I told him 'sure.' I told him I don't have any claim on you and you can go out with whomever you want. I'm sorry, Hilary," said Eddie, looking down at her with his sky-blue eyes. "I don't mean to hurt you. It's just over, that's all. I want to start going out with other girls."

"You mean Mimi?" asked Hilary.

"I don't know. Well, I guess so. Yeah, I guess I would like to go out with Mimi. We can still be friends though. I've got to go now. I don't want to keep my brother waiting. Bye," he said. Eddie turned and ran down the sidewalk and slid into the front seat beside his brother. The engine started and the car disappeared into the night.

Hilary stood on the porch for a few minutes, breathing heavily. What a disasterous night! What a horrible evening, Hilary thought. She felt like her insides were caving in. The evening had begun with her going steady with Eddie. She had been dressed up just like Eddie asked her to be. They'd giggled and talked on the way to the dance. And now it was all over. Now she wasn't Eddie's girl anymore. It all ended so quickly and without warning.

Hilary opened the door. Her mother was already in bed. Hilary climbed the dark steps to her room. She pulled off her clothes and climbed into bed. She didn't wave through her window at Mrs. Suffington like she did on every other night. Tonight was different.

Hilary pressed her face into her pillow and the tears began to come. She felt like she was the most alone person in the world. Even Mrs. Suffington, alone in her house for twenty years, couldn't feel any more alone than Hilary felt tonight. She felt as if she would be alone for the rest of her life. She didn't want to go out with anyone but Eddie. No one could take his place . . . no one.

Hilary Weathervan cried herself to sleep. She dreamed that she was in a room looking out through a dusty window. Outside, the whole world was dancing and laughing. All she could do was stand back and watch. She was alone and no one knew and no one cared.

Eight

THE next Monday at school was torture for Hilary. Eddie wasn't waiting by her locker in the morning, and he didn't meet her between classes to carry her books. Everyone was talking about the new girl from New York. Everyone commented on her short hair and how cute it was, and on her clothes, and how stylish they were. Everyone was saying the same things about Mimi that they used to say about her when she first moved to Suffington. But the worst time came at lunch.

After third period, Hilary usually walked down to the cafeteria and met Eddie at their special table by the window. They had sat there together for every lunch for the past month. But today was different. Hilary didn't rush down the stairs to the cafeteria. She didn't want to get there before Eddie did. She didn't want to go to "their" table and wait and wait for Eddie, only to find out that he wasn't going to come. All the kids would see her sitting there waiting for him. They'd either feel sorry for her or they'd laugh at her. Either way she couldn't stand it.

Hilary waited in the bathroom. She stood in a stall so that no one could see who she was or how red her eyes were from a weekend of crying. She listened to the sounds of girls chattering and laughing in front of the mirror. Girls traded lip glosses, borrowed safety pins, and compared Saturday night dates. A voice reached Hilary that she didn't recognize, so it had to be one of the eighth graders. The girl said, "It was a super party! Everyone danced and Michelle had some great albums." Her voice sunk to a whisper. "Did you hear about Eddie Stoner and Hilary Weathervan?" she asked.

"No," came the response.

The first voice continued, "They broke up at Michelle's. I saw it happen. Hilary was real upset, but then what do you expect from a seventh-grader? She should have known that Eddie's the type of guy who likes to change girl friends. I found that out a long time ago," she said with a sigh. "Maybe now she'll quit being such a snob and thinking she's so neat just because she's from a city."

"I think Eddie Stoner's a jerk," came a voice from someone by the bathroom sink. She turned the water off and continued to speak.

"I didn't think Eddie would drop Hilary the way he did. I thought he liked her a lot. That's a pretty jerky thing he did, even if Hilary is kind of a snob."

Hilary recognized the voice as Jerry Dapple's. She couldn't believe that Jerry was saying that she, Hilary Weathervan, was a snob. Also, she couldn't believe that anyone could think that Eddie Stoner was a jerk. Wasn't he captain of the Junior Varsity football team? And wasn't he the cutest guy with the bluest eyes in the junior high class?

"Well, if you ask me, Hilary's got a lot to learn," said another voice. "We'll see how she likes it now without Eddie to lead her around like a little puppy dog. Only at first did she even try to make friends with any of the girls here. You'd think that the only person she thought was good enough for her in the whole school was Eddie."

"Some girls are like that," said the eighth-grader. "All they care about are boys and they don't care about having any girl friends."

Hilary felt tears rising to her eyes. She couldn't believe what was being said about her. It hurt. It was as if everyone in the school hated her and she didn't even know it until now. All of a sudden she had gone from being very popular to being the biggest snob in Suffington. She heard a flurry of activity out in the bathroom. The girls were leaving.

"Let's go to lunch, okay?" asked the eighth-grader. "I'm meeting Angie at the big table by the front door. Want to sit with us?"

"Sure," came another voice. "Let's go."

The door opened and the group of girls left the bathroom. Hilary put the toilet lid down and sat on it. She put her face in her hands and tried to choke back a sob. She wished that she was home in her bedroom, safe and far away from all these kids who hated her, safe from Eddie who didn't love her anymore. But wishes don't always come true, and Hilary knew that she had to go to lunch in the cafeteria. Anyway, maybe Eddie had changed his mind. Maybe he was waiting for her in the cafeteria like he always did.

Hilary made another wish. She whispered to herself, "Oh please, please, please let Eddie be waiting for me. Please let me sit with Eddie at lunch." Hilary opened the stall door and walked out into the empty bathroom. She looked at her face in the mirror and took a compact from her purse. She dabbed powder over the pink, puffy skin under her eyes. Hopefully, no one could tell that she had been crying. Taking a deep breath, she hugged her purse to her chest and left the bathroom.

She made her way through the crowded hall and descended the stairs to the cafeteria.

When she walked in the door she looked over to "their" table to see if Eddie might be waiting for her. For the hundredth time that day, Hilary's stomach twisted into a knot. At "their" table sat Eddie and Mimi. Eddie looked as happy as a lark. He looked like he'd never even known or cared for a girl named Hilary. He sat there smiling and talking to Mimi as if she were the only girl in Suffington.

Hilary looked around and saw Jerry, Pam, Bonnie Jean and Dan Ellsworth sitting at a table. They were the only people that she knew in the whole cafeteria. Could she sit with them? After all, Jerry thought that she was a snob. Probably the others did, too. But Hilary just couldn't face the thought of sitting at a table alone. Everyone would stare at her and talk about how Eddie had dumped her. She walked toward Jerry, Pam, and the gang.

"Hi, everyone," Hilary said, trying to sound cheerful.

They all looked up at her in surprise. "Hi," said Bonnie Jean.

"Can I sit with you?" asked Hilary. She felt so stupid. She felt as if she had some awful disease and no one wanted to be anywhere near her.

"Sure," said Dan. "Have a seat."

Hilary sat down, placing her lunch bag on the table beside Dan's. Everyone was staring at her as if she had two heads. Could they tell that she'd been crying? She tried to think of something to say. She turned to Dan and said, "You know, I've been thinking about that writer's job on the *Sentinel*. If it's still open, I'd like to have it. Does anyone have the job yet?"

Dan looked uncomfortable. "Well . . . " he said. "It's still open. But to tell you the truth, I don't know if you're the person for the job."

Hilary's sandwich began to shake in her hand. "Why?" she asked. "I'm a really good writer. I know I could do a good job."

"I'm sorry, Hilary," said Dan. "But the newspaper staff needs someone dependable. We need someone we can count on. You had that football writing assignment a couple of months ago and you never finished it. We ended up having a blank space in the paper and we had to rush around at the last minute to find an article to fill it."

Hilary couldn't believe that this was happening to her. It was as if her whole world was falling apart and no one cared or wanted to help her.

"I've got some poetry at home," she said. "I could bring some in for you to read. Then you could decide if I write well enough to work on the *Sentinel*," she said.

Dan squirmed in his seat and looked around

at all the people at the table. No one else said a word. "I'm sorry, Hilary," Dan said, again. "I just don't have time right now. I'm trying to get that section on phobias and medical problems together for the paper. Also, the English class is sponsoring an essay-writing contest and I'm one of the judges. That's keeping me busy. I wish I could look at your stuff, but right now I just don't have the time. Sorry."

"What are phobias?" asked Bonnie Jean. Hilary could tell that she was trying to change the subject.

"Phobias are fears that people have," said Dan. "They're fears that are so strong that they can wreck people's lives."

"Is there such a thing as a cafeteria food phobia?" asked Jerry. The others laughed and Hilary managed a smile.

"There are all kinds of phobias," said Dan. "Some people have phobias about being in high places, or being in crowded rooms. Some people have phobias about taking tests. They get all bent out of shape when they have to take a test, even if they know the stuff. It's just that taking tests makes them super nervous. A phobia is any kind of fear that gets so huge that a person can't deal with it. It's a fear that interferes with a person's normal life."

Hilary thought, I wonder if there's such a thing as a life phobia? My life has changed so fast that I don't like it. I wish I could just go to sleep and wake up when everything was better. I wish I could trade my life for someone else's.

Hilary wondered who she'd like to trade lives with. Out of the corner of her eye, she looked over at "their" table. It was empty now. Eddie and Mimi must have left together, she thought. Oh, why can't I trade lives with Mimi? It hurt Hilary to think that Eddie and Mimi were somewhere together right now. It hurt to think about what they might be saying to each other and whether or not they might be holding hands.

The bell rang and Hilary hurriedly left the lunch table and was off to her next class. She felt like a volcano that was ready to erupt. She wondered if all the rushing students around her knew that she was ready to explode. It was weird to feel so alone in the middle of a crowd.

* * * * *

Edith Weathervan reached over and stroked Hilary's head. "How did school go today?" she asked. "Did you see Eddie?"

"Yeah," said Hilary. "He ignored me all day. Everytime I saw him he was with Mimi."

Hilary's voice choked. It seemed that every time she thought about Eddie, tears came rushing to her eyes. "What am I going to do, Mom?" she asked. "I feel so alone. There's no other guy I want to date. When I was with Eddie everyone thought I was something special."

"I think you're special," said her mom.

"Thanks, Mom," said Hilary. She didn't want to tell her mom that it wasn't enough to be thought of as "special" by her own mother. Most girls wanted to be special to a guy. They wanted a guy to hold their hand on wintery nights and take them to parties. A girl needed a guy to look at her with sparkles in his eyes and tell her that she was different from all the other girls. A girl needed a guy like Eddie. At least, *this* girl did.

"I think I'll go up to my room," she said. "You said that hard work would make me feel better. I feel so crummy right now that I'm willing to try anything. I have a poem that I started a long time ago. I think I'll finish it tonight."

"Okay," said her mom. "If you feel like talking, just let me know."

"Thanks, Mom," said Hilary. She walked up to her room and switched on her desk lamp. She dug through her papers and found the poem that she had begun after her first meeting with Mrs. Suffington. She looked at the title, *A Lonely Heart.* Suddenly, it took on new meaning. When she had first begun it, she had been thinking about Mrs. Suffington. But now, her own heart was the lonely one. She picked up her pen and began writing. The words seemed to come so easily, now that she knew what it was like to feel forgotten and unwanted. She wrote:

A Lonely Heart

When I'm alone inside my heart,
I yell and scream to let you know
That I'm alone and I'm afraid.
I'm too afraid to let fear go.

With doors and heart locked tight with keys,
I sit alone inside myself.
I feel no sun or summer breeze
Like a china doll on a dusty shelf.

I'm waiting and waiting for someone to
   come,
And rescue me from my darkest hours.
He'll take my hand and kiss my cheek
And lead me down a path of flowers.

Hilary reread the poem. It captured all her feelings of loneliness. She began to think of Mike back in Philadelphia. He may not have been as cute or exciting as Eddie, but at least he was always there. Hilary wondered if it was too late to write to Mike. Maybe he would forgive her for breaking up with him. Maybe he would take her back. Then again, maybe he had a new girl friend by now. Then there was always Judd Grolling. It might be better to go out with Judd since Mike lived hundreds of miles away.

Hilary thought about the different boys in her class whom she knew. Maybe she could start talking and getting to know some of them. Even Dan Ellsworth wasn't too bad of a guy. He was better than no one at all, even if he didn't want her writing for the school newspaper.

Hilary leaned her head on her hand and thought about how unfair life was. She thought that once people fell in love with each other they should be in love with each other for the rest of their lives. Why didn't love last? she wondered. If only love could last forever, then her mother would still be married to her father, and Eddie Stoner would still be going steady with her.

But that's not the way it was. Life got so scrambled and tangled sometimes. One minute you were holding hands with a boy who said he liked you, and the next minute you were hiding in a bathroom stall listening to people talk about how that same boy had dumped you. Oh, it was just too much! she thought. If only love could last! A tear slid down Hilary's nose and fell on her poem.

Hilary had a sudden thought. What about Mike? she remembered. She had dumped him when he wasn't expecting it. How could she blame Eddie's love for not lasting, when her love for Mike hadn't lasted either? She wasn't the only person in the world to feel the pain of a break up. Mike had felt it. Her mother and father had felt it, too. Mrs. Suffington had felt it when her husband died. Probably, everyone in the whole world got left behind at least once in their lives.

Hilary wondered who would be the new boy to enter her dreams? Who would be the one to take her on hayrides and dance with her after football games? Another tear slid down Hilary's nose and splashed against her poem. Hilary remembered a pair of sky-blue eyes and reached for a tissue.

The phone rang downstairs and Hilary jumped at the sound. The ringing stopped which meant her mother had answered it. Could it be Eddie? she wondered. Maybe he had decided Mimi wasn't nearly as much fun as she was. Maybe he missed her and wanted to get back together.

"Hilary! Hilary!" came her mom's voice from downstairs. She was yelling excitedly.

Hilary jumped up and ran from her bedroom and down the stairs. "What is it, Mom?" she asked. "Who's on the phone? Who is it?"

A happy smile beamed from her mother's face. "You'll never believe it," she said.

"Who?" asked Hilary.

"It was Eric Lawrence from the office," she said. "He's the Products Manager in my division. He's asked me for a date. We're going out to dinner this Saturday. He says there's a beautiful little restaurant in Westchester, near here." She smiled happily. "He thinks that I'm one of the best market analysts around. Oh, Honey, I'm so excited! This will be my first date since your father and I were divorced."

"Great," said Hilary, without enthusiasm.

Mrs. Weathervan looked closely at her daughter. "Honey," she said. "This doesn't upset you, does it? It's just a date. Can you handle being alone here this Saturday? I promise I won't be gone too late. Maybe you could ask some of your girl friends over."

"I could if I had any girl friends," moaned Hilary.

"Oh, Hilary. Now come on! You know that if you would just make a little effort you'll have just as many friends here as you had in Philadelphia," her mom said.

"I didn't have any friends there either," said

Hilary. "Just Mike."

"Honey, I hate to say this, but it sounds like you're feeling sorry for yourself. You know, the world goes on after you break up with someone. Life goes on."

"Gee, thanks for the pep talk," said Hilary.

"I mean it," said her mom. "Some people meet someone and they're friends forever. Or they get married to someone and they're married to that person forever. And that's wonderful for those people. They learn from their long friendships and from their long marriages. But there are other people who have friends coming in and out of their lives, and they learn something from that, too. You can learn from loving people and being able to let them go when the time comes for that."

Tears welled in Hilary's eyes. "That's easy for you to say," she said. *"You've* got a date and *I'm* the snob of Suffington Junior High School, sitting at home on a Saturday night with no friends and nothing to do."

Edith Weathervan wrapped her arms around Hilary and held her against her chest. "I love you so much," she said. "Your father loves you and I'm sure the kids in this town will love you, too, after they've gotten to know you better. There's love all around you. But right now you don't seem to love yourself very much, and it's hard for you to see the sunshine just around the corner."

"Where's the corner?" Hilary sniffled, pulling away from her mother.

"You reach the corner when you go on with your life," her mom said. "You learn about yourself and you learn about the things that you love to do, and you do those things. Then you feel good about yourself. After that, it's really kind of easy. Once you love yourself, you're ready to love the rest of the world."

"All that I love to do is write," said Hilary.

"Then write," said her mom. "If that's what makes you feel good about yourself, then do it."

"Okay," said Hilary. "I don't have anything else to do. I don't have any friends so I guess I'll just hole up in my room and write for the rest of my life."

"That's a beginning," her mom sighed. She smiled and said, "I wonder what I should wear this Saturday. How about that black dress with the silver belt?"

Nine

"I'M sorry, Hilary," said Jerry. "I'd like to spend Saturday night with you, but we have an away game. My mom's taking me and Pam and Bonnie Jean. I'd ask you to come, but there's no more room left in the car."

"Oh, well. Maybe some other time," said Hilary, forcing herself to smile. "See you later."

Well, that's what you get for trying to be friends, Hilary thought to herself. She walked out to the bus and got on. Riding home on the bus after school was the pits. She sat in an empty seat because everyone else had a friend to sit with. Everything in her life seemed to be going from bad to worse, she thought. She was doomed to a Saturday night alone at home. *Even her mother had a date.* And the only three girls she knew in the whole school couldn't spend the night because they were going to the basketball game. At least, that's what they said they were doing.

Hilary spent Friday night writing poetry. She wrote a piece called *Give Me a Break,* and one called *A Weekend in Prison.* Then her hand began to get a cramp in it, so she went to bed even though it was only 8:30.

Saturday afternoon came and brought with it freezing rain and hail. Little balls of ice banged at Hilary's window as she sat at her desk writing a short story. It was about a young girl named Esmeralda Lilac who built a boat from an old picnic table. Then Esmeralda Lilac sailed away to a deserted island where only monkeys and beautiful tropical birds lived. The monkeys loved Esmeralda very much and gathered flowers and fruit for her. Esmeralda Lilac danced in the moonlight and swam in the surf with her good monkey friends. She had it made.

When Saturday evening came, Edith Weathervan waltzed out of her room in a sleek black dress with a shining silver belt. "How do I look?" she asked Hilary.

Hilary looked at her mother with astonishment. "Mom, you look great!" she said. "Wow! I didn't know you could look so good."

"Thanks . . . I think," her mom said.

"Just one thing," said Hilary. "Why don't you wear some makeup? I've got some cherry-crimson lip gloss that would look great on you."

"Oh, Honey. You know I don't like to put that gook on my face. Eric can take me to dinner, pale lips, wrinkles, and all!" she laughed.

The doorbell rang and Mrs. Weathervan rushed to answer it. She opened the door and a medium-tall man with brown hair and a moustache stepped in. "Hello, Edith," he said. "Are you ready? Oh, this must be Hilary, the writer. Hello there, Hilary. I've heard a lot of good things about you from your mother." He smiled and held out his hand for Hilary to shake.

Hilary shook his hand and looked back at him. He wasn't too bad looking, she thought.

"Hilary, we'll be in Westchester. I left the number of the restaurant by the telephone. There's plenty to eat in the frig. Have a good time, Honey." Her mom leaned over and kissed her daughter. Then she and Eric walked out of the front door. Hilary watched them from the living room window as the car's headlights disappeared into the dark winter night.

The house seemed huge and empty. Hilary heard a board creak upstairs. That was one of the bad things about living in an old house. The boards creaked and the furnace hissed in the basement. Those sounds weren't so bad when someone was with you. But when you were alone, the noises sounded like they could be alien creatures or strange monsters made out of bad dreams. Hilary realized that she was starting to get scared by listening for strange noises. So she tried to think of something to do. She didn't want to write anymore because she'd spent Friday night and Saturday morning doing it and she was sick of it. So she decided to try on clothes.

As she looked in her closet, she saw the green and white dress that she'd worn the night that Eddie broke up with her. She decided that she didn't want to try that one on ever again. So she took the dress off the hanger, folded it up, and stuffed it into an empty boot box. Then she tried on a cute red skirt that she hadn't worn in a while. If she ever had a date again, she'd wear it for sure. Hilary tried on a few more outfits. Then she tried on every shoe in her closet and realized that there were four pairs there that she hadn't worn in almost two years. Then she put on a shiny cornflower blue eyeshadow, purple liner, and strawberry pink lip gloss.

Hilary leaned toward her dresser mirror and felt that her made-up face looked ready for a party. All of a sudden she wanted to be with someone. She was tired of being alone. She wanted someone to see her colorful and bright makeup. She wanted to be with someone who wanted to be with her. But she was alone in a big, old, empty house and she hadn't a friend in the world. Suddenly, Hilary knew what it was like to be Mrs. Suffington.

She caught her breath at the thought of Mrs. Suffington alone and forgotten in that big, dark house. Mrs. Suffington was probably feeling just as alone as Hilary was right now. She would probably love to hear Hilary's special knock at her front door. Mrs. Suffington had told Hilary to use the special knock so that she would know who it was. Then she wouldn't be afraid that it was a group of hooligans on the front porch. The special knock was two quick taps, then wait for two seconds, then one loud knock.

Hilary pulled on her boots and ran to her closet for a jacket. It was too bad that Mrs. Suffington didn't have a telephone. Then Hilary could have called her to tell her that she was coming over. But the way that Hilary felt right now, she didn't know if she could have waited to dial a telephone. In just two minutes, she had on her boots, gloves, jacket, and scarf and was racing out the front door. She slid on the front walk and had to grab onto a bush to stop. Then she ran into the yard, and back by the side of the house to Mrs. Suffington's yard.

Knock . . . Knock . . . pause . . . KNOCK!

Hilary waited. She heard a movement within the house. Then a creaky high voice said, "I'm coming, Hilary."

A moment later, Mrs. Suffington opened the door and Hilary hugged her. "I'm glad you're home!" she said. Then she remembered that Mrs. Suffington was *always* home, and she laughed.

"Come in, child. Come in," said Mrs. Suffington. "You'll catch your death of cold out there. I just put on a pot of tea."

That was funny. It seemed like every time Hilary came over, Mrs. Suffington had just put on a pot of tea. She must drink about a million pots a day.

Hilary followed Mrs. Suffington into the parlor like she always did, and sat on the red velvet sofa. It seemed kind of funny to be visiting Mrs. Suffington on a Saturday night, Hilary thought. Saturday nights were supposed to be for going out with boyfriends or girl friends.

Mrs. Suffington lifted the china teapot and poured two steaming cups of tea. She handed one to Hilary and said in her quivering, high voice. "Why aren't you out with Eddie tonight? I've noticed the light's been on in your room a lot lately. Did you two have a lover's quarrel?"

"We're not seeing each other anymore," said Hilary with a sigh. "Eddie found a new girl."

"Oh, dear! I'm sorry to hear that," said Mrs. Suffington sympathetically. "He must be a very silly young man to hurt a nice girl like you. But then I think most of the young men today are hooligans."

"I don't know," said Hilary. "Maybe it's my fault for not being pretty enough or exciting enough. Maybe I'm just a dud."

"Oh, pooh!" exclaimed Mrs. Suffington. "That's foolish talk! My husband, Uriah, used to say that there are two kinds of boys. One kind knows how to be friends with a girl, and the other kind thinks girls are like Cracker Jack prizes."

Hilary thought about that. Maybe she had been Eddie's Cracker Jack prize. Maybe she'd been just a cute girl wearing stylish dresses that Eddie could show off at parties. And now Mimi was his new prize.

Hilary settled back into the sofa cushions and sipped her tea. The winter winds howled outside. It felt good to be indoors sharing heart-talk with someone who cared about her. It felt good to reach out to someone who was just as lonely as she was. Perhaps two lonely people together could take away each other's loneliness, even if it was just for a little while.

"I'm so happy that you came to visit," said Mrs. Suffington as if reading Hilary's mind. "It gets pretty lonely here in this big, old house, now that Uriah's gone."

"Why don't you leave?" asked Hilary. "I'd go nuts if I stayed cooped up all the time. Wouldn't you feel better if you got out and learned to be with people again? Wouldn't you like to get out and see what's going on in the town?"

"Oh, heavens!" cried Mrs. Suffington. "I'd never! All those people. They're just out to get you, if you ask me."

"No, they're not," said Hilary. "*I'm* out there and *I'm* not out to get you, am I?"

"I suppose not, dear," said Mrs. Suffington. "But it's a crazy world. I think I'm safer tucked away here. More tea?"

As Hilary held out her teacup she heard a sound. It was hard to hear it because of the screaming winds outside, but she definitely heard it. Mrs. Suffington heard it, too. She cocked her head to one side and listened. "What is it?" Hilary asked. A look of fear came over Mrs. Suffington's face. "Oh, no, not again," the old woman mumbled to herself.

Suddenly there was a crashing noise. KABLAM! Hilary jumped up from the sofa. Mrs. Suffington put her hands to her chest in alarm. "It's them again," she said. "They've come back. They always do."

"Who?" asked Hilary. "*Who* are they? And *where* are they?"

"It's the hooligans," whispered Mrs. Suffington. "They come in through the basement window. The wind blows it open. They come in right through that window and they try to scare me by making terrible noises in the basement."

As if on cue, a high pitched shriek rose from the ground under them. E-e-e-o-o-owww-eee! came the noise. Hilary felt the back of her neck tingle. "Hooligans?" she whispered. Suddenly, Hilary took Mrs. Suffington's hooligan stories seriously. Maybe some of the kids in the neighborhood were trying to scare her. It made Hilary shiver to think of the pranksters hiding in the basement. Who were they? Why did they want to scare a little old lady who lived all alone?

E-e-e-o-o-owww-eee! The shriek came again. Mrs. Suffington's cup of tea fell to the floor with a clatter and tinkling of broken china. "Oh-oh-oh. I can't take much more of this," she said.

As Hilary watched the look of fear on Mrs. Suffington's face, her own fear turned to anger. What kind of mean person would scare an old lady like that? she wondered. Hilary was mad. She walked toward the door that led to the basement.

"What are you doing?" asked Mrs. Suffington. "You're not going down there, are you? The hooligans may hurt you!"

"Yes, I am," said Hilary. "We've got to make them stop." The sound of something being knocked over from the basement below reached their ears. Hilary was afraid. But she was determined to catch the kids in the act. She opened the basement door and felt a gust of cold air. She felt along the wall for a light switch. "Where are the lights?" she whispered.

"There aren't any," murmured Mrs. Suffington. "This is an old house. There aren't any lights in the basement. You'll have to use a candle. Are you sure you want to do this. Those hooligans are waiting down there."

Hilary wasn't so sure that she wanted to descend into that strange, pitch-black basement with just a candle in her hand. But she'd already said that she would, and she didn't want to back down. She had to go down there.

Mrs. Suffington handed a candle in its holder to Hilary. The flame flickered and danced in the cold air currents that flowed from the darkness below.

"Here goes nothing," said Hilary. Carefully, she placed her foot on the top step. C-r-e-a-k. Oh, these old houses and their creaking floorboards! she thought. At this rate, she could never sneak up on anyone. They'd hear her coming a mile away. Slowly, she took another step, then another, and another. Mrs. Suffington stood, trembling, at the top of the steps. As Hilary descended into the basement, the light from upstairs grew dimmer. She was surrounded by blackness, with just a small circle of yellow candlelight shining on her hand and casting wavering shadows on the boxes and old furniture stacked in piles around her. She turned quickly as she heard a movement in a dark corner. Someone was hiding.

Hilary's heart pounded. She'd never been as afraid in her life as she was right now. Here they were, two people alone in a big house with someone or something hiding in the darkness, trying to scare them. A box moved and Hilary almost dropped her candle. She squared her shoulders and walked toward the noise. She had to walk around an old chair. She peered into the darkness and with a skip of her heart, she saw a patch of something white moving behind an old sewing machine. "Who's there?" she yelled in a voice that was much stronger and braver than the way she felt on the inside. "Come out, right now! Who are you?"

The white patch moved again and Hilary leaned toward it, stretching the candle out into the darkness. Suddenly she caught the flash of two bright yellow eyes beaming from the black basement corner. A tiny pink mouth opened, showing a line of sharp, white teeth. "Oh!" Hilary gasped. "It's a cat!"

"E-e-e-e-ow!" came the cat's cry. It arched its spine and hissed at Hilary. She backed away, afraid that the cat might leap into the air and scratch her in its fright.

"Hilary! Are you all right?" came Mrs. Suffington's quaking voice from the top of the stairs. "Have you caught the hooligans?"

"It's just a cat!" called Hilary. "It's just a little gray cat with a patch of white on its chest." She peered more closely at the cat who crouched under a chair and stared back at Hilary. In the candlelight she could see that the cat's ribs were sticking out. It looked as if if hadn't eaten in days. It was little and scrawny.

A cold gust of air burst through the open basement window and the cat shivered. Hilary climbed on top of a table and closed the window. It was cold in the basement, but not as cold as it was outside. This poor little cat was just trying to get out of the stark wintry night and find a warm place to cuddle up. It needed help, and it needed someone to love it. Hilary smiled. Maybe some sixth sense had told the cat that this house was where the lonely hearts club was meeting on this cold Saturday night.

Hilary set down the candle and tried to pick

up the cat. Suddenly the cat ran up the stairs and into the house.

"Mrs. Suffington, the cat just ran into the house! Do you have any milk?" called Hilary. "This cat's starving."

"I've got something better than that," said Mrs. Suffington. "I've got some cream. I always have plenty on hand for my tea." She went to the kitchen where she poured thick white cream into a little saucer.

Hilary looked everywhere for the cat. When she found it, she led Mrs. Suffington to the old chair in the corner of the kitchen where the cat remained huddled. "E-e-e-ow-eee!" it howled. "Poor thing," said Mrs. Suffington. "It's all skin and bones." She handed the saucer of cream to Hilary who set it on the floor and pushed it toward the cat. The cat's ears perked up and it darted toward the bowl and began lapping the cream as fast as it could with its little pink tongue.

"Well, here's your 'hooligan,' " laughed Hilary, winking at Mrs. Suffington. All this time you thought hooligans were hiding in your basement, but it was just cats coming in to get out of the cold."

"Come to think of it, there seems to be more hooligans in the winter and during the April rains," said Mrs. Suffington. "Maybe I've been running a hotel for cats and I didn't even know it." She clapped her hands together with pleasure. "You know what?" she exclaimed. "That's a wonderful name for a cat. Let's call it 'Hooligan.' "

"Hooligan," Hilary murmured to herself. "Hooligan. That's a good name."

The gray- and white-patched Hooligan lapped up the last few drops of cream and licked the saucer clean. Hilary knelt by the chair and held her hand out to Hooligan. The cat's eyes widened in fear, but it looked curiously. Hilary lowered her hand slowly to the cat's head and gently scratched it behind the ear. Immediately, a loud purring sound came rumbling from the depths of the scrawny creature. It moved its head against Hilary's fingers, begging for more love. "Sweet, sweet, little Hooligan," Hilary whispered to the cat. "Welcome to The Lonely Hearts Club." The cat purred at the sound of Hilary's voice.

Hilary slowly put her hands around Hooligan's body. Gently, she lifted the cat. It felt like a little ragdoll. It lay quietly in Hilary's arms as she put the cat in Mrs. Suffington's lap. "Nice kitty," said Mrs. Suffington, stroking the cat's fur. Mrs. Suffington looked closely at the cat. "Well, I do believe we have a little girl on our hands," she said. Hilary peered at Hooligan. "Yup," she said. "Hooligan's a girl all right."

"She's a girl who needs fattening up, too," said Mrs. Suffington. "Uriah used to always say that girls get too skinny when they're not being love enough. I'd say that Hooligan here needs some food and love, wouldn't you?"

"For sure," said Hilary. "Want me to get some more cream?"

"Certainly," said Mrs. Suffington. "I'll sit here with Hooligan."

Hilary filled the bowl with cream, then set the bowl on Mrs. Suffington's lap. Hooligan stood up and eagerly lapped the cream. When she was done, her motor came back in full force. "I can feel her purring," said Mrs. Suffington. "Hooligan's purr goes right through my dress and into my lap. It's like I have a dress full of bumblebees, but none of them have stingers. What a lovely sound. I think Hooligan's telling us that she loves us."

Hilary watched Mrs. Suffington's wrinkled face soften. The cat lay in a curl among the folds of Mrs. Suffington's dress and suddenly, Hilary wouldn't have wished to be anywhere else in the world. Here she felt safe in the cozy, old house, listening to the crochety voices of winds rattling at the shutters outside. A cream-filled cat purred in the lap of a tea-filled old woman who had just discovered that her hooligans were really nothing more than the scratchings of cats' feet. Hilary had discovered something, too. She discovered that a Saturday evening spent without a date can make you brave enough to explore dark, creepy basements.

Ten

MONDAY morning came and Hilary dressed for school feeling like a lion tamer preparing to walk into a cage full of ferocious beasts. The beasts were all the students in Suffington Junior High. It didn't seem fair to have to spend five days a week in a school full of kids who didn't like her. Hilary ate breakfast quickly, said "good-bye" to her mother, then hurried out to catch the bus. She walked to the back of the bus where she sat alone in a seat.

At school, lockers slammed and voices called out to each other. But no friendly voices called out to Hilary. It was as if she didn't even exist. She tucked her books under her arm and hurried off to English class. At the last bell, she took her seat.

Mrs. Covert, the English teacher, stood at the front of the room with a smile on her face. "Good morning," she said cheerfully. "I've got some good news for those of you who like to write. All of the English classes are sponsoring

117

a writing contest for the whole school. Your entries are to be no more than three pages long. The deadline for entries is in two weeks and the judges will call you if your entry wins. We'll be giving prizes for the first-, second-, and third-place winners at an awards ceremony before the whole school. I encourage all of you to enter.

Hilary listened with interest. At last this was her big chance! Maybe she could win the contest and then all the people in school who didn't like her would notice her. They'd find out that she, Hilary Weathervan, was something more than the ex-girlfriend of Eddie Stoner. She, Hilary Weathervan, was a girl with brains and talent. She was a great writer who was going to be famous someday. When the people found that out, they'd all want to be friends with her.

Hilary remembered that Dan Ellsworth had said that he was one of the judges for the contest. He'd used that as an excuse to get out of reading Hilary's poetry. Hmmm-mmm, she thought. If Dan was going to be one of the judges, what would he like to read about? Phobias, she remembered. That was it! Dan said that he wanted to do a section in the *Sentinel* on phobias. If she entered an essay on phobias, Dan would have to read it since he was one of the judges. He'd love it as if it was an article for the paper. Hilary spent the rest of English class thinking about the contest.

The day wore on. When it came time for lunch Hilary walked into the cafeteria, looking around for someone to sit with. Eddie and Mimi sat together, as usual. Dan, Pam, Jerry, and Bonnie Jean sat at a table. Angie and Michelle were pinching each other and giggling at another table. Hilary took her lunch bag and sat at an empty table.

"To heck with them," she said to herself. If they don't want to be my friends, then I don't want to be their's. But, they'll all think differently when I win the contest.

Hilary smiled to herself and pulled out a sandwich from her bag. She felt like a wallflower sitting there alone. She felt like she should be wearing a T-shirt that said "I Am A Dud" on front of it. She suspected that the people around her were looking at her and thinking about what a snob she was. But she'd show them that even snobs fight back. They'd find that out during the awards ceremony when she would be on stage receiving her award for first place.

Hilary choked on a piece of sandwich and had to spit it out into her napkin. Gross! Hopefully, no one saw her do that. What a nerd I am! she thought.

At home that night, Hilary ate her dinner as

fast as she could. "What's the rush?" her mother asked.

"I've got to get started on my essay for the writing contest," Hilary said. "I've just got to win it."

"That's wonderful, dear," her mom said. "I'm glad to see that you're getting back into your writing. But, be careful that you don't set yourself up for a disappointment. Don't set your heart on winning first place, okay?"

"I'm going to win," said Hilary. "I've just got to. I'm going to write about phobias. Phobias are terrible fears that people have. I've just got to figure out what kind of phobia to write about."

"How about the fear of people?" suggested her mom. "Maybe Mrs. Suffington could help you with that one."

"Mom! That's a GREAT idea!" cried Hilary. "I could interview Mrs. Suffington about what it's like to be afraid all the time. Maybe if she talked about it with me, she'd learn not to be so afraid of people." Hilary jumped up from the table. "Can I go over to Mrs. Suffington's?" she asked breathlessly.

"After you do the dishes," Mrs. Weathervan said.

"Aw, Mom. I'm inspired. Great artists shouldn't have to do boring stuff like dishes and housework," Hilary complained.

"Off to the kitchen, Shakespeare," said her mom with a grin.

Hilary carried dishes to the kitchen sink where she plunged them into warm, soapy water. As she rinsed bowls, she daydreamed about Esmeralda Lilac, the girl who lived with monkeys on a deserted island. How wonderful it would be to have trained monkeys wash dishes for you. When the last dish was set in the drainer to dry, Hilary ran to find her jacket and gloves. "I won't be gone long, Mom!" she called, and ran out into the night.

Knock . . . Knock . . . pause . . . KNOCK! Hilary tapped out the code on Mrs. Suffington's front door.

Floorboards creaked as Mrs. Suffington answered the call. "Coming, Hilary," she said. The door opened and Mrs. Suffington stood there in a black dress and pink shawl. "Hilary, dear!" she exclaimed. "I'm so glad you dropped by. I just made a pot of sassafras tea. Would you like a cup?"

"Sure," said Hilary. She followed Mrs. Suffington into the parlor, where Hooligan lay like a gray ball of fluff on the red velvet sofa.

"Hooligan, dear. We have a visitor," said Mrs. Suffington. Hooligan stretched and yawned.

"She doesn't look too excited about it," laughed Hilary, scratching Hooligan behind the ear. Hooligan purred contentedly.

"Oh, she just thinks she owns the place," said Mrs. Suffington. "Feel her belly. I've never in my life seen a cat eat so much!"

Hilary told Mrs. Suffington about the writing contest at school, and she told her about the essay she planned to do on phobias. But it was harder to explain to the gray-haired woman that she planned to write about her. How would Mrs. Suffington feel about being the subject of an article about fears? she wondered. She was a woman who had spent the last twenty-two years living in private. How would she like for her life story to become public?

Hilary decided to come right out with it. "Mrs. Suffington," she said. "I wondered if I could interview you for it." Hilary breathed deeply and looked at Mrs. Suffington.

The wrinkled face frowned slightly. "You know, Hilary, dear. Uriah used to say that there are two sides to every coin. Maybe you could find a subject for your essay closer to home. Do you know what I mean?"

"I'm not sure," said Hilary. "Do you mean that you don't want me to write about you?"

"Oh, no, no. That's not what I meant at all," said Mrs. Suffington. "You can write about me if you want to. But all I'm saying is that Uriah used to say that every coin has two sides."

She's 82 years old, Hilary thought to herself. Sometimes she doesn't make sense. It probably comes from spending so much time alone because she's afraid of people. Maybe I can use that in the essay. Hilary pulled out her notebook and a pen. "Mrs. Suffington, how does it feel to spend so much time alone? Don't you ever wish that about a million people would come over and bring a stereo and records and food? They could dance and have a party all over your house? Don't you hate being alone on Saturday night?"

"Heavens!" Mrs. Suffington exclaimed. "A house full of hooligans? Dancing? I think I'd have to throw water on them to make them leave!" She pressed her hand to her heart.

Wow, is she paranoid, Hilary thought to herself. She put pen to paper and began to write.

* * * * *

On Wednesday, Hilary spent another lunchtime alone in the cafeteria. She was getting used to it. These days she brought a book along with her so that she could pretend to be reading. That way it looked like she didn't want to sit with anyone. It looked like she wanted to be alone. Today was better than usual because she really did have something to work on. She had her essay for the contest.

"Hi, Hilary." Hilary looked up to see Judd Grolling standing with his lunch tray behind the empty chair across from her. "You look pretty busy. Mind if I sit down?"

"Sure. Yes. I mean, no. Sit down," she mumbled. The words tumbled out of Hilary's mouth.

Judd sat down. "What are you writing?" he asked.

"It's for the essay contest," she said.

"Oh, really? Boy, lots of people are entering that. So am I," he admitted with a grin.

Hilary was surprised. "What are you writing about?" she asked.

"Football," he said. "I figure that's the only thing that I really know something about. I'm going to write about how scary it is to know that there are a bunch of guys out there who are ready to jump on you and knock your brains out when you have the ball. The other guys will probably call me a chicken. But I swear, I'm afraid every time I get out there. You really have to psych up yourself."

Oh, no, thought Hilary. He's writing about fear. That's kind of like my essay. But mine's about phobias.

"You know, Hilary," said Judd. "I've been watching for you at the basketball games. I go to most of them. I never see you there. Aren't you into basketball?"

Hilary didn't want to tell Judd the real reason. She never attended the games because no one ever asked her to go with them. "I've been pretty busy," she said.

"Oh, do you have a boyfriend that I don't know about?" asked Judd with a smile.

Was this embarrassing! "Kind of," said Hilary, mysteriously. She pulled her essay paper closer to her and began writing so that Judd wouldn't ask her anymore questions.

Judd stood up and said, "I'm sorry I bothered you." He walked away and sat at a table with some other guys from the football team. Hilary felt her face blushing pink. Judd used to have a crush on her, but now he was rejecting her just like everyone else.

"Why do I always manage to say the dumbest things?" she asked herself. Why did she tell him that she had a boyfriend? She just didn't want him to know how alone and friendless she was. She didn't want him to know that she was the sort of girl who spent Saturday evenings in dark basements with starving cats and scared old ladies. Hilary peeped over at "their" table. Mimi was dropping a buttered roll down Eddie's shirt. They were both squealing with laughter.

* * * * *

"Zip me up, please, Hilary dear," said Hilary's mom. "Are you sure this dress doesn't make me look fat? How does my hair look?"

"I thought you didn't care about stuff like that," said Hilary. "I thought you said Eric could accept your gray hair, wrinkles, and all."

"Well, a woman should take pride in her appearance," she said. "There's no harm in that, is there?"

It was Saturday evening, and Hilary's mom had another date with Eric Lawrence. Hilary didn't mind quite so much this time because she was eager to spend an evening working on her essay for the contest. So far, she'd only written one page and it just didn't sound like first-prize material. Something was wrong. She had interviewed Mrs. Suffington five times, and still she couldn't work the information into an essay.

"Help me, Mom, before you go," said Hilary. "You've read my essay. How can I improve this thing? I'm drawing a blank."

"I'd advise you to look closer to home for a story," said her mom. "A writer should always write about something that they understand. You know, there are two sides to every coin."

This was weird. Those were the same words that Mrs. Suffington had used during her first interview, Hilary recalled.

The doorbell rang and Mrs. Weathervan left

on her date with Eric. Hilary climbed the stairs to her room and turned on her desk lamp. She waved through the window at Mrs. Suffington out of habit, even though Mrs. Suffington didn't lurk at the windows now that she had Hooligan. Hilary kind of missed knowing that the old woman could always be counted on to be there watching by the window. Now, even Mrs. Suffington had someone to keep her company, and Hilary had no one. Once again, she was at home alone on a Saturday evening and hating the fact that she was the only person in the whole world with absolutely zero friends. Not only that, but everyone kept telling her weird stuff like "There are two sides to every coin."

Suddenly, Hilary understood what everyone was talking about. She saw both sides of the coin. One side was Mrs. Sufferington and her phobia of being WITH people. The other side was Hilary and her phobia of being WITHOUT people. Mrs. Suffington was afraid of togetherness, and Hilary was afraid of loneliness. The topic for Hilary's essay had been close to home after all. Mrs. Suffington may have been hiding from people in her house all these years because of her fear. But Hilary had been hiding, too. She had hidden first behind Mike, and then behind Eddie. She, Hilary Weathervan, was afraid to be alone, she suddenly realized.

"What was so awful about being alone?" she asked herself. The questions whirled in Hilary's head. Why was she so afraid of loneliness? Did being alone mean that you were unpopular and no one wanted to be with you? Did it mean that if you were alone today, then you would be alone tomorrow, too, and every day for the rest of your life? Did it mean that no one would take care of you? Did being alone mean that you had to take care of yourself? Was that why she was afraid to be alone, because she was afraid she'd have to take care of herself? Hilary remembered the afternoon that she had hidden in the bathroom stall and listened to an eighth-grade girl say that Hilary followed Eddie around like a puppy. Had she loved Eddie just because he took her to parties and made her feel popular? Did she love him because he took care of her? That seemed just as jerky as Eddie dating her because of her miniskirts and triple-pierced ears.

Hilary tore up her essay and pulled out a clean sheet of paper. The words came easily now and she could hardly write fast enough. *Afraid To Be Alone* was the title that she gave her essay. It was certainly a subject that she knew something about.

Eleven

HILARY spent the next two weeks writing and rewriting. It was hard to keep the essay down to three pages because she had so much to say about being afraid to be alone. She felt like an expert on the subject. Hilary walked to classes alone, ate lunch alone, and rode the bus home from school alone.

Her mother had another date with Eric on Saturday and Hilary was glad that at least her mother had found a good friend in Suffington. There was no point in both of them being unpopular and lonely. Besides that, Eric was a nice guy, and he even asked Hilary to come to dinner with them. But Hilary said, "No thanks. I need to finish this essay. The deadline is Monday."

When Saturday evening came, Hilary sat in her room writing. She put the finishing touches to her essay and breathed a sigh of relief that it was done. But part of the evening still stretched in front of her and she wasn't

sure what to do with herself. She thought
about running over to Mrs. Suffington's, but
decided that she had to learn to spend an
evening at home alone. After all, she had just
written an essay about how important it was to
spend time with yourself. But what else was
there to do besides write?

Dancing! That was it! Hilary went down to
the kitchen where there was a radio. She
turned it on and tuned in a good rock station.
She closed her eyes and listened to the music.
She felt the beat of the rhythm and began to
move in time to the music. It felt good. Hilary
danced all around the kitchen. The music grew
faster and Hilary whirled and twirled. She
jumped onto a kitchen chair where she stood
shaking her shoulders and rolling her head.
"Boy, if anyone could see me now, they'd think
I was weird," Hilary said to herself. Then she
laughed out loud. "But who cares? So what if
I'm a little weird? Weird can be fun." Hilary
jumped from the chair to the floor and did
splits.

When Monday came, Hilary turned in her
essay to Mrs. Covert. She saw a big stack of
contest entries sitting on the desk. Hopefully,
hers would be the best of the bunch.

"Class!" Mrs. Covert called. "The judges
will begin looking at all the entries this
afternoon. A winner will be chosen by this

Wednesday and one of the judges will call you if you've won. The awards will be presented at a school ceremony this Saturday evening. Good luck to you all!" Hilary crossed her fingers.

When Wednesday came, Hilary stared at Mrs. Covert in English class, trying to see if the teacher would give away any clues as to who the winner was. But she didn't, and Hilary rode the bus after school that day, still not knowing if she was to receive first prize in the contest.

"Calm down, Honey," said Hilary's mom. "If you win, you win. But don't be disappointed if you don't. You know, everyone can't be a winner."

The phone rang and Hilary ran to get it. Maybe this was it! "Hello?" she said breathlessly into the phone.

"Hilary? Hi. This is Dan Ellsworth."

Hilary gasped at the sound of his voice. Her eyes widened and she grinned into the phone. "Yes?" she said.

"Hilary, that was a great essay you wrote," said Dan. "The judges really like it. You've won third place."

"Oh." Hilary couldn't keep the disappointment from her voice. "Third? Who got first and second?" she asked.

"That will be announced at the awards

ceremony," said Dan. "That will be in the school auditorium this Saturday at 7:30. You'll be there, won't you?"

"Sure," said Hilary. "Thanks. Bye." She hung up the phone.

"Who was it?" her mom asked.

"I won," said Hilary.

"Oh, Honey! That's wonderful! Hey, what's the problem? You don't look very happy," her mom said.

"I won third place," moaned Hilary.

"But you won! That's great!" she added.

"Yeah. I guess so," said Hilary. She felt funny. She felt happy and sad at the same time. It was great to win the contest, but she had set her heart on winning first place.

"Eric will be so pleased," said her mom. "I know he'll want to come to the ceremony and watch you receive your award. We'll have to do something to celebrate. Won't that be nice?"

"Yeah. Sure," she mumbled. I guess I should be happy with third place, she thought. Some kids didn't win at all. She went up to her room. The more she thought about the ceremony, the more excited she became. Just think! She would be up there on the stage and the whole school would be watching. At last, everyone would know Hilary Weathervan! She'd have to look her very best. What should she wear? How should she look? she wondered.

When Saturday came, Hilary tried on every dress in her closet, but none of them seemed to look quite right. She peered into her closet and her eyes fell on a boot box tucked away in the corner. She opened it and found the green and white dress that she'd worn when Eddie broke up with her. She unfolded the dress and shook out the wrinkles. "Well, why not?" she asked herself. "It's a nice dress. I'll wear it." Suddenly, the dress seemed like an old friend that Hilary hadn't seen in a while. She put it on and it looked great. Then she sat down before her makeup mirror and put on the brightest makeup that she had . . . purple liner, mauve eyeshadow, navy mascara, and strawberry ice lip gloss.

"Good heavens, Hilary," her mother said when she saw her. "Your face looks like a rainbow."

"Thanks, Mom. Are you ready to go yet? Are you ready to see your darling daughter get her prize up in front of the whole school?"

"My! You certainly have perked up," she laughed. "Nothing like a little success to get rid of the blues, huh? Eric is picking us up. He'll be here any minute."

"Great!" said Hilary. "I'll need lots of fans in the audience."

Moments later, Eric pulled up in front of the house. Mrs. Weathervan and Hilary rushed out and climbed into the car. "Congratulations, Hilary," said Eric. "I know how hard you worked on that essay. I'm proud of you."

Hilary leaned back into the backseat with a satisfied grin.

"Oh. One more thing," said Eric. "Is it okay if I drop you off at the school? I need to drive your mom over to the office to sign some papers. It'll just take ten minutes. We'll get back in time to see you up on stage. Don't worry. I wouldn't miss it for the world."

"Don't worry, Honey," her mom added. "We won't be gone long."

Oh, wow. This was too much! Hilary thought. Her own mother wasn't going to walk into the school with her on her big night. Once again, Hilary had to go it alone. Eric pulled up in front of the school. Hilary got out and slammed the door shut behind her. The car drove off and Hilary was left standing alone on the sidewalk while other kids walked with their parents into the school. Hilary mumbled to herself, "I know it's okay to be alone sometimes, but this is getting ridiculous." She climbed the steps to the front door and headed toward the auditorium.

The auditorium was a huge room with rows

of seats and hundreds of people chattering and moving around. It seemed like the whole town was there.

Hilary walked into the crowd. She moved to the front of the auditorium and took a seat. Mr. Weaver, the principal, walked out onto the stage. Voices quieted and people took their seats. The lights dimmed and Hilary felt her stomach do somersaults as she realized that her mother and Eric would never find her in the dark.

"Good evening," boomed Mr. Weaver. "Welcome to Suffington Junior and Senior High School. We come together tonight to honor three of our school's finest writers. We had many entries in the Suffington Essay Contest, so it was difficult to select the winners. But I believe that the three essays chosen by our judges were the very best out of the whole school.

"Let's begin by calling up our first-place winner. She's a new student in our school and we're proud to have her . . . Mimi Trost. Would you please come to the stage to receive your first-place award?"

Everyone in the auditorium began clapping. Everyone, that is, except Hilary. She sat in her chair, staring in disbelief as Mimi, in a bright yellow miniskirt, walked down the aisle and climbed the steps to the stage. It had to be some kind of mistake. Surely, first place for writing couldn't be going to Mimi. Not the Mimi from New York! Hilary thought. Not Mimi, who's going steady with Eddie!

"You've done a fine job, young lady," Mr. Weaver said. He shook Mimi's hand and gave her a piece of paper and a blue ribbon. "Mimi's essay was called *New York — The City of Skyscrapers.* Let's have another round of applause for our first-place winner," said Mr. Weaver into the microphone.

Hilary listened to the clapping and cheering around her. Was it her imagination or could she hear Eddie yelling from somewhere in the back of the room? Oh, where was her mother when she really needed her? she wondered. Hilary craned her neck around to see if her mother was standing somewhere near the door. Nope. She wasn't there. Hilary turned around and faced the stage once more.

"Our second prize ribbon goes to Mike Jarvis. Come on up here, Mike." The clapping began again, as a blonde-haired boy walked toward the stage. Mr. Weaver continued to talk into the microphone. He said, "Mike has written an essay called *The Martians in My Attic.* I got a chuckle when I read it. Mike, you didn't REALLY see Martians in your attic at home, did you?" Mr. Weaver smiled and winked at the audience.

"Just once," said Mike. He took the paper and red ribbon from Mr. Weaver's hand and began to leave the stage.

Mr. Weaver looked a little surprised. He said to the audience. "Well, you know what great imaginations these writers have. Let's have a round of applause for Mike."

Hilary had to laugh in spite of herself as she clapped. This Mike seemed like a funny person. Maybe he would be someone worth getting to know. Anyone who could write about Martians in his attic had to be pretty interesting.

"And now, it's time for our third-place winner. Miss Hilary Weathervan. Please come up to the stage!"

Hilary felt her back tense. It was her turn at last. Everyone was waiting for her to walk up to the stage. She looked around for her mother, but didn't recognize any faces in the dark auditorium. Her legs felt like licorice sticks as she walked down the aisle and climbed the stage to face Mr. Weaver.

"Hilary has written an essay called *Afraid to Be Alone,*" Mr. Weaver said. "I agree with the judges that this was a very good and sensitive piece. It captured the feelings that a young girl has when she spends a lot of time alone. Well done, Hilary." Mr. Weaver handed her a paper certificate with her name on it, and a green ribbon. The audience clapped.

Hilary smiled and shook his hand. She winced at the thought that now every kid at Suffington knew that she didn't have any friends.

"Hilary, I understand that you brought a special guest with you tonight," Mr. Weaver said.

Hilary blushed. "My mother was coming, but she had some work to do at the office," she said. How embarrassing. Now all the kids would know that even her own mother didn't like her enough to come to the awards ceremony.

Mr. Weaver chuckled. "Is Mrs. Weathervan out in the audience?" he called. His voice boomed around the large room.

"I'm here!" she called.

"Someone turn up the lights!" yelled Mr. Weaver.

The lights became bright and Hilary stared out from the stage into the crowd of people.

"Here we are!" she called again. She waved her hand from the middle of the room. Hilary stared. There they were. There was her mom, Eric, and Mrs. Suffington. Hilary's eyes almost popped out of her head. Mrs. Suffington! There she stood in her old black dress and pink shawl. Her white hair floated around her face like a cloud. "Mrs. Suffington!" Hilary exclaimed into the microphone. "What are YOU doing here?"

Mrs. Suffington said something, but Hilary couldn't hear what it was. The whole audience began talking and turning their heads to stare at Mrs. Suffington.

"Mrs. Suffington, we welcome you," said Mr. Weaver above the din. "We're proud to have a member of Suffington's first family here with us tonight. It's been a long time. Welcome."

Hilary ran from the stage. She ran down the aisle back to where her mother, Eric, and Mrs. Suffington sat. She tripped over feet and knocked into knees as she edged down the row and threw her arms around Mrs. Suffington. "Oh! I'm so glad you're here!" cried Hilary. Then Hilary released Mrs. Suffington and hugged her mother and Eric. "Mom, you're something else!" she cried. "You were really leaving to go get Mrs. Suffington, weren't you?"

Her mom smiled shyly. "I wanted it to be a surprise, Honey. Sorry, we were late."

"We were late because of me," choked Mrs. Suffington. "I don't move as fast as I used to. And Hooligan wanted to come, but I had to sit down and have a little talk with her."

"Once again, congratulations to our winners, Mimi, Mike, and Hilary. That's all for tonight,"

Mr. Weaver called out to the audience. "We'll have coffee and punch in the gym. Good night, everybody." He left the stage, and the crowd in the auditorium began to leave. On their way out, people approached the Weathervans to congratulate Hilary and to welcome Mrs. Suffington back into public life.

"Hey, Hilary!" Hilary looked around to see Dan Ellsworth weeding his way through the crowd. "Hilary," he said, "I've got to talk to you."

Hilary stopped and faced Dan.

"Hilary," he said. "I want to know if you want to write for the school paper. Your essay was really good. I was impressed."

"I'd love to write for *The Sentinel*," said Hilary with a smile. She held her hand out to Dan who shook it. "Looks like we'll be working together now, won't we?" asked Hilary.

"Yeah," said Dan. "It should be fun. Hey, about that day in the lunchroom when I said you couldn't work on the paper . . . I hope I didn't hurt your feelings. I was under a lot of pressure, and really, I just didn't have the time to read your poetry. Now that the contest's over and you're writing for the paper, I wonder if I could take a look at them. I'd really like to see what you've written."

"Sure," said Hilary. "No problem. Want to come over Monday after school?"

"Sure," said Dan. "I'll meet you at the bus." He disappeared into the crowd.

Hilary felt someone squeeze her hand. She turned to find Jerry Dapple standing by her side. "Hilary," Jerry said. "Congratulations!" She lowered her voice to a whisper. "Dan let me read your essay. It was really good. Seriously, I didn't know that you were lonely. I thought you *liked* being alone. And I thought that you didn't want to be friends with anyone else except for you-know-who."

"Eddie?" asked Hilary. "That's all over. I guess it'll hurt for a while, but I'll live." She grinned at Jerry, and at Bonnie Jean and Pam, who had just squeezed their way through the crowd. "I've discovered how important it is to like myself, and I've learned how important it is to reach out to friends and let them know how I'm feeling. I guess I had to do it on a piece of paper first," she laughed.

"Welcome to Suffington, friend," giggled Jerry. She squeezed Hilary's hand again.

The crowd left the auditorium and Hilary rode home with Eric, her mother, and Mrs. Suffington. Later that night, alone in her room, she thought about the day's events and how her life had suddenly gone from being dark and dreary to being filled with sunshine and promise. Dan was coming over Monday, and Jerry, Pam, and Bonnie Jean wanted to be friends with her. It was wonderful!

Suddenly, Hilary felt like dancing. There was no music to guide her steps. There were just the sounds of January winds singing outside, and boards creaking as the old house settled down for a long winter's night. But Hilary felt the music in her heart. It was a song of happiness that came with feeling confident about oneself. It was the song of life, and it was coming in loud and clear, filling Hilary from head to toe.

Hilary Weathervan twirled across her room with her nightgown flowing around her. She spun three times and landed in a ballerina's curtsy. "Wow! I didn't know I could do that!" she said.